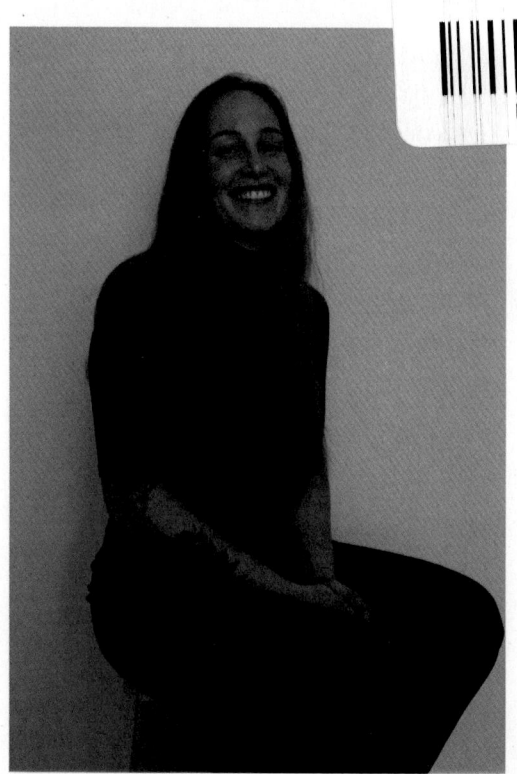

About the Author

She is an animal lover by heart who loves to travel the world and she is always up for new adventures and enjoys going wherever life may take her. She always strives to have fun and come up with new challenges for herself, which can be anywhere between learning how to climb, or spontaneously choosing to write a book while exploring the coasts of Africa.

The Last Septarian

Cecilie Odgaard

The Last Septarian

Olympia Publishers
London

www.olympiapublishers.com
OLYMPIA PAPERBACK EDITION

Copyright © Cecilie Odgaard 2023

The right of Cecilie Odgaard to be identified as author of
this work has been asserted in accordance with sections 77 and 78 of
the Copyright, Designs and Patents Act 1988.

All Rights Reserved

No reproduction, copy or transmission of this publication
may be made without written permission.
No paragraph of this publication may be reproduced,
copied or transmitted save with the written permission of the publisher,
or in accordance with the provisions
of the Copyright Act 1956 (as amended).

Any person who commits any unauthorised act in relation to
this publication may be liable to criminal
prosecution and civil claims for damage.

A CIP catalogue record for this title is
available from the British Library.

ISBN: 978-1-80439-261-4

This is a work of fiction.
Names, characters, places and incidents originate from the writer's
imagination. Any resemblance to actual persons, living or dead, is
purely coincidental.

First Published in 2023

Olympia Publishers
Tallis House
2 Tallis Street
London
EC4Y 0AB

Printed in Great Britain

Dedication

This book is dedicated to every young boy and girl out there with the desire in their hearts to one day write a story of their own. And remember, the only way to truly fail at something is to never even try.

    I am also dedicating this book to the man I love and to my lovely friend, Silke, who both supported me every step of the way and sat by my side as I went on the journey to write this book.

Introduction

Some treasures are real while others are pure myth, and some treasures are even somewhere in between the two. For as long as there has been treasures in our world, there has also been guardians around to keep them safe, and for as long as treasures have been lost, treasure hunters have been on the lookout attempting to find them.

This, however, is not a story that revolves around the guardians nor the treasure hunters. This is a story about two young troublemakers, and as most people are aware of, troublemakers tend to get themselves into trouble, and occasionally even with the wrong crowd, which is exactly what happens to the two main characters in this story, Kleo, and Matt.

The two of them always get each other into trouble and eventually find themselves on the journey of their life, running against time, trying to find what is said to be one of the most valuable and dangerous treasures of all, before it falls into the wrong person's hands.

But how did it all begin?

It began centuries ago with nothing less than a septarian. You see, there was a time, long before our own, where mystical creatures wandered the Earth. There are many theories to where they came from, if they even existed, or why and how they disappeared, and if some might even still be around to this day. Many of these creatures are said to have died millions of years ago, during an asteroid impact, where only few are expected to have survived, if any. Many of the creatures were, according to myth, discovered by humans later on and hunted down one by one, and within almost no time, the little proof of them ever existing, was completely gone. Some believe that the creatures fled in order to hide themselves, deep inside the forests, in the shadows of the caves and some even hid in the depths of the ocean. Whether some are still alive and hiding out there today, no one truly knows for sure.

And what is a septarian you might be wondering?

The only way to truly figure it out, is to be a part of the adventure, and go on the journey along with Kleo and Matt.

Chapter One

The sun was peaking in the sky, the water was slowly flowing down the stream, the leaves on the trees were dancing as the touch of the wind gently glanced through them while the birds, resting in their nests, could be heard piping away. It was all peace and quiet until the interruption of two young people who were sword fighting, making their way throughout the forest disturbing the nature with the sound of their swords constantly rambling together.

"Give up," yelled a young man.

He held a black, yet shiny, sword in his hand and had a wooden bow and arrows strapped to his back. He was strongly built, with a strong jaw, brown eyes, dark hair, and light clean skin. He was wearing leather pants, shoes, and a white button up shirt along with a loose leather vest. His name was Matt, he lived in one of the villages outside the main town and was known to be somewhat of a troublemaker. He had a heart of gold and had always been one to stand up for what he believed in.

"I'm not a quitter," said a young woman back with a rather fierce voice.

This was Kleo. She was a very beautiful young woman, with sapphire blue eyes, a beautiful dark skin and with long cornrows reaching all the way down to her hips. She was thought to be a true fighter and was also the darling of her village. She had been practicing sword fighting ever since she was a child. Her sword was given to her by her late father, it had a decorated golden handle with a long thin blade. She was always wearing pants and a shirt along with a tight leather corset as armor. Her mother always tried to have her wear dresses and be a proper lady, but Kleo found that dresses were not really practical for fighting and she preferred pants and a good shirt any day of the week, even if it did not soothe her mother.

The two of them were always practicing with their swords at every chance they got. They were practicing so that they would always be prepared for every scenario they could possibly come across. They fought for hours, both refusing to give up despite being almost out of energy. After a while as they were both exhausted from wielding the heavy swords, they started to get sloppy and did not really watch where they were going. They were approaching a stream, which neither of them seemed to have paid attention to, and before they knew it, Kleo fell into the water, and Matt followed right after.

"Thank god the water isn't deep," Matt said to Kleo with a cheeky smile on his face, as he knew she feared water and did not know how to swim.

Her father used to be a fisherman until he died at sea when Kleo was a still a young child. He drowned in the ocean when his ship went under, and he had not had anywhere to escape.

Matt on the other hand never knew either of his parents. He was handed to an orphanage when he was a newborn and had lived there his entire childhood, until one day when he was finally old enough to take care of himself.

"Let's call it a tie today, Matt," Kleo responded with exhaustion, and Matt instantly agreed.

After they got out of the water the sun was almost setting. They walked through the forest to get back to the village, all while discussing what trouble they should get into next. You see,

Matt liked to get into trouble, let alone dragging Kleo with him. There was always something to steal or something to make a mess of. Not from the villagers of course, but from the men causing trouble around the area. Kleo and Matt usually stole supplies from them to use for their adventures or geared up with arrows to practice their aim in the forest. One time they had even stolen a few of their horses, just to go for a ride, and later set the horses free on the other side of the forest.

Matt always did his best to keep Kleo out of the more dangerous 'missions' and he was always very protective of her, not that she could not fend for herself, but in the last couple of years he could not deny that he had grown very fond of her, and he could not bear the thought of anything ever happening to her.

The two of them had known each other almost their entire lives. Back then, the trouble they got themselves into was not quite as dangerous as opposed to now. Matt used to sneak out of the orphanage at dusk, going to the markets to see if there were any fruits to steal, or maybe some tools to snatch, that he could use to make small wooden soldiers for him and his friends at the orphanage.

One day, he had gone to the market, the same market where Kleo was. She was there helping her mother who worked for one of the farmers. They were setting up a stall where they would sell big fresh pumpkins that grew on the fields each year around October. As Kleo was sitting on a bench inside the stall, bored, waiting for something to happen, she spotted a boy walking around looking like he was up to no good. The boy, of course, was Matt.

She could not help but wonder what he was up to, so she had, without further thought, decided to follow him. You see, Kleo was an expert in staying unseen when she wanted to which in this occasion had proven to, once again, be a handy skill to have. The boy was walking up behind a big pile of apples and as he was just about to grab one of them, a voice behind him said

"That's called stealing you know," it was Kleo being cheeky as she walked up behind him.

Matt obviously got a shock and accidentally dropped the apple, that he had just stolen, on the ground. As he turned around, he was met with the sight of a girl, with beautiful big blue eyes, staring right at him.

Kleo picked up the apple, she looked at it and continued talking, "If you want to steal an apple you might as well take one of the good ones, this one is half rotten already."

Matt looked confused. Was she trying to catch him or help him?

She went over to the pile of apples and looked around with a rather quirky look on her face. She grabbed two of the best-looking apples in sight, gave one to Matt, and the other she took for herself and bit off a huge chunk and smiled at him.

Matt was just about to introduce himself to her as they got interrupted

"Thieves!" yelled a man who had seen the two little children take his apples.

Matt and Kleo ran away as fast as they could. They maneuvered their way in between all the people in the market and continued onto a huge cornfield, where they would be hard to spot, and hid in between the tall crops. After a while they stopped to check behind them if they had gotten away. There was no man in sight, and he was not to be heard yelling for them any longer. They were safe and they luckily still had the apples in their hands.

"My name is Matt," he said while smiling to her.

"Pleasure to meet you Matt. I'm Kleo."

Ever since that day they had been inseparable. They had even made a deal with each other to meet up every day and practice sneaking, stealing, and fighting and they had both remained true to their words.

***

They had reached the village where they both had lived their whole lives. It used to be smaller, but over the years many more families had moved there and therefore more houses had been built. It was soon to be a proper town. The village even had a school for the children, where they could be taught to both read and write.

Most of the houses were built from wood, had low rooftops with small chimneys sticking out. Only a few of the larger houses were made from stone and belonged to the wealthier families where most of the men were a part of the king's army.

The villagers primarily consisted of farmers, butchers and blacksmiths who survived by transporting and selling their goods to the larger towns.

In spite of the village growing, it was no longer as lively and colorful as it once was. The streets used to be filled with the sweet sound of live music while children were running around freely playing games with one another. The markets were filled with the sight of fresh fruits, vegetables and the smell of freshly baked bread came from the bakery every morning. In the evenings the people of the village used to gather at the center where they would dance all night long until their feet could no longer carry them, all the while enjoying warm meals together.

All that was gone.

Ever since the fires and plunderings had started a few years ago, the mood of the city had turned gloomy. However, they still had it better than the people living in the other villages and towns.

Kleo and Matt walked past the local tavern where one of the elderlies sat outside every evening telling all his different made-up stories and fairytales to the children on the streets.

Yesterday the story had been about fairies and how they would steal your teeth during the night when they were asleep and today, he was telling a story about dragons and how they used to rule the world.

"Do you think it's true?" Kleo turned to Matt and asked as she liked the idea of dragons and how magnificent they seemed to be.

"No, and if it was true, I certainly would not care to meet one," Matt said. "He's just an old man who is too fond of beer making up stories to scare the children, as usual," he continued while trying to have her scoot along and stop listening to the man's nonsense.

Further down the streets, as they passed an alley, they overheard two drunk guards talking. They were no guards of the village nor were they a part of the king's men. These were the ones who participated in the plunderings and burned down the houses in the area.

Matt stopped and stared into the alley at the two men while he tightened his fists.

"Matt, no," Kleo said trying to get him to move along but it was too late. He was going into the alley, and she went right after him.

"Are you lost," Matt said in an attempt to provoke the guards.

The men looked at Matt and chuckled. "Sorry, darling, we don't fight little girls."

Kleo interrupted them, "Are you saying that women can't fight?" she asked the men while lifting her clenched hands.

The men laughed even harder. They could not believe that a young woman wanted to put up a fight with them.

"Oh. You shouldn't have said that," Matt said with an almost excited look on his face.

Before the men even had a chance to react Kleo threw a hard knuckle into the face of one of the guards. Matt followed right after, throwing a punch at the other. Even though the two men did their best to fight back, it did not take long before both of them were on the ground, sore and unable to say anything but sounds indicated that they were in great pain.

And just like always, Kleo and Matt left unharmed.

They had always considered themselves quite lucky, no matter what mess they had gotten themselves into they had never been caught and always managed to leave unharmed.

It was getting late, and it was time for them to part their ways, go to their homes, and get some rest. Kleo lived with her mom in a small house in the outer part of the village and Matt lived in the other end with one of the toy makers in the village. He had lived there ever since he left the orphanage and usually helped out building some of the wooden toys. Before they said goodnight to each other they had decided to meet up again in town after midnight, to see if they could cause some trouble, especially now that they knew that the men were in the village again.

***

They always met up in the same spot, right behind the local butcher shop. Here there was an alley perfect for a hideout.

Nobody ever went there because of the stench and the rats crawling around. It was awful. The ground in the alley was covered with bones from the animals butchered in the shop along with leftovers of rotten meat that could not be sold.

Even Matt and Kleo had a hard time dealing with the smell, so they usually covered their mouth and nose with a scarf. It was the only place within miles that none of the guards ever went, or anyone else for that matter, so here they could hide until they were ready with their plans.

They needed more arrows for Matt's bow, as some had broken in the fight from earlier with the two drunk men, and what better way to get arrows than to steal them from the men tormenting the villages? They were ready and as they moved out from behind the butcher shop, they heard someone talking not far from where they were standing. It sounded as if it came from the next street, so they decided to climb on top of a house to get a closer look. Kleo went first and climbed to the roof being as stealthy as she possibly could. She reached the top in no time and carefully looked around to see who was talking. They were right beneath her but thankfully they had not noticed her moving around above them. Matt followed right after her, and as he climbed up towards the roof, he accidentally banged his sword onto the wall of the house making a huge bumping sound. The talking immediately stopped. Kleo ducked as far down as she could, hoping they had not yet seen her. In the meantime, Matt hurried to climb the rest of the way to hide on the roof.

The noise had disturbed the men and they were about to walk around the house checking if someone was spying on them. Just as they reached the backside of the house, Matt had reached the roof and was out of sight. The men stayed quiet for a short while, listening closely, in order to figure out if they were alone or not.

After, what seemed to be only a few seconds, they continued talking to one another.

"Bring it with you tomorrow at midnight and meet me here," said one man to the other before they both left, each going their separate ways.

"Bring what?" whispered Kleo to Matt with an intrigued look in her eyes.

"I have no idea," he replied being as confused as she was. "But there's only one way to find out."

Chapter Two

It was nearly midnight, and the town was quiet. The streets were dark as there were no lights besides a few small candlelights flickering in the windows of some of the houses. The only sounds to be heard, throughout the otherwise silent night, was that made from the small gusts of wind blowing through the narrow streets and dogs barking in the distance.

Oh, and of course footsteps and the clanking sound of armor moving throughout the night. The footsteps came from the intruders in the town. Nobody would walk the streets at night risking running into any of these men.

The men were under orders from a man named Enzo. Enzo was known to be a heartless man with no other intentions than that of becoming the wealthiest and most powerful man, no matter the cost. It was him and his men that had been tormenting the town and surrounding villages for years and were now slowly making their way into the town.

Him and his men were known for robbing and stealing valuable items from around the world in exchange for gold pieces. There were rumors going around town saying that he was there searching for something, something to lead him on the way to power. However, nobody seemed to know exactly what it meant or what it was that he was searching for.

In the other end of town, the man from yesterday was meeting up with some of Enzo's guards. They exchanged only a few words before they were given something wrapped in parchment and in return the man got a big bag of gold before he quickly disappeared into the night.

Little did they know that across the streets behind a barn were Matt and Kleo. Even though neither of the two had heard any of the words that were spoken, they had still witnessed the whole thing. They looked at each other with their eyes agreeing that whatever was in that piece of parchment, they had to get their hands on before it reached Enzo. For, with the amount of gold the man received, it had to be something of great importance.

Matt and Kleo followed the men while staying in the shadows, trying their best to remain unseen. They had decided to use the tactics they themselves called 'distreat'. Which was really just a combination of distract and retreat, but they seemed to find the name rather funny.

The name of the tactic was something they had invented when they were young kids, trying to steal cookies from the local bakery. Matt would walk in and distract the baker while Kleo would walk around through the back and steal the cookies before quickly retreating without being noticed.

"Which one of you are up for an ass beating? Or are you all as weak and afraid as you look?" Matt asked with a sassy expression on his face while staring the men in their eyes as he drew his sword.

The men looked at each other smiling as they all drew their swords and took a few steps towards Matt. They did not seem to care much for his threats, but they were definitely up for teaching him a lesson. One guard had walked all the way up to Matt's face, staring down at him hoping that it would scare him off, however, it did not work well since Matt threw a punch right in his face which caused his nose to start bleeding. The other two guards quickly grabbed Matt by his arms and tightly held onto him and pushed him hard onto the ground. Just as they turned their backs away, Matt quickly got back up on his feet and fenced his sword towards the guards. They got ready to fight him as he was clearly refusing to give up. Just as they all started fighting in the middle of the streets, Kleo snuck up behind a house and scouted to see which of the guards held the piece of parchment.

She quickly noticed that one of the men had it strapped to his belt and slowly approached the fight while staying out of sight. Matt noticed Kleo in the corner of his eye and tried to lure the men closer to where she was hiding, so that she would have a better chance at snatching the parchment. Kleo saw her chance as all the men were facing Matt. She slowly and silently drew her sword, approached the guard, and made a quick cut to his belt, causing it to fall to the ground along with the parchment. The man got surprised and as he quickly turned around, he went for Kleo with his sword. Her sword blocked his right before it hit her face. Her eyes were in shock. It was a close call. She fought back with all she had while Matt kept the others entertained.

The fighting continued and they knew that they needed to come up with a solution if they both were to get away in one piece. Matt tried to lure them towards some barrels close by. The barrels were filled with oil. If he could just get them close enough and pour the oil on the ground, they would have a head start to retreat as the men would hopefully use a second or two sliding around, or at least be distracted long enough for them to run off. A few hard strikes with his sword and Matt was now right in front of the barrels. He jumped on top of one of them and tried to tip over the one next to it, however it was too heavy for him. Kleo was struggling to distract the men as they started to approach Matt. He had to think fast since one of the men was right in front of him and was about to come at him with his sword. Matt jumped back down on the ground, struck his blade into one of the barrels as hard as he could and yelled for Kleo to cover her eyes.

He pulled the sword out quickly and swung it in front of the men's faces, getting the oil from the sword to spray into their eyes. As they were all blinded, he ran to Kleo, grabbed her arm with one hand and grabbed the parchment from the ground with the other before they ran away as fast as their feet could possibly carry them.

"That was a close call," Matt said to Kleo right before they were stopped by a group of horseback riders.

It was Enzo and his men.

They must have heard the fight from afar and approached to see what the fuss was about. Two of the men jumped down from their horses and pointed their swords towards Matt and Kleo. They knew they were outnumbered so it was not wise to pick a fight. They had no other choice but to surrender.

"They are coming with us," Enzo said while turning his horse around getting ready to ride away.

Kleo looked at Matt with fright in her eyes. What was going to happen now?

Fortunately, Enzo did not find the parchment as Matt had hidden it inside of his clothes right before they were caught. The men took away their weapons, bound Matt and Kleo's hands with rope and forced them to walk behind the horses all the way to Enzo's territory.

As they arrived at the fort, they were thrown into two separate dungeons. Matt called out for Kleo to hear how far away she was; however, he did not get any response. He tried to call out a few more times, hoping that he would hear her voice in the distance, yet still no response was to be heard.

He started to worry, searching the room for a way out. There was nothing helpful, only some flint stones on the floor and a tiny window with bars in the far top corner of the room that were too tiny for him to fit through anyway. He reached for the parchment inside his clothes but stopped for a second to check if any of Enzo's men were close by. He was alone so it was safe to take a look at what they had stolen. He opened the knot on the rope that held the parchment together and slowly folded it out. His eyes got big with amazement and he could barely believe his own eyes. It was not something wrapped in parchment. It was the parchment itself that was of value.

He heard footsteps at the end of the hall from some of Enzo's guards that were approaching. He could not let Enzo see what he had just seen. He knew he did not have time to get rid of the whole thing without them noticing, so he tore off a big piece, grabbed two flints from the ground, and started to make sparks to light it on fire. It did not take long for the parchment to burn and the other piece he rolled back together as fast as he could and hid in his clothes. Just as the guards stood in front of the cell the last embers from the burning parchment went out.

The guards opened the door to his cell and one of the men looked at him with a grin on his face before he threw a hard knuckle right in Matt's face and then dragged him out into the hallway. He was dragged throughout the hall and all the way up the stairs that led outside, there he was pushed into the building across the street and almost thrown through the doors, where he then fell to the ground. As he tried to get up, he heard a laugh.

"Get up boy," Enzo said.

Matt looked up at him with disgust while getting back up on his feet. Enzo was sitting upon what looked like a throne, but he was no royalty. Matt looked around but could not spot Kleo anywhere.

"You have something that belongs to me. Hand it over and I will leave your friend unharmed," Enzo said with a very serious and dead look on his face and he could tell that Matt was looking around for Kleo.

"Where is she?" Matt said with a stubborn voice. He knew he could not hide from the fact that Enzo was aware that he had the parchment in his possession since the men he stole it from were in the room with them.

Enzo ignored Matt's question. "You have something of mine, give it to me now and I will let you see your friend," he said with an impatient voice.

Matt stared at him with loathing and did nothing. He refused to give him anything without knowing that Kleo was unharmed. Enzo looked back at him with a smirk and shouted to two of his men in the room next door.

"Bring her in here!" he yelled to Whitefoot and Shirtless who was on the other side of the door keeping an eye on Kleo.

This of course was not their real names, but nobody seemed to remember what their real names were anymore, after having called them only by their nicknames for years. Whitefoot got the name, since he, for some reason, always wore two different colored boots. One was dark brown, and the other was as white as milk. Why he wore it, nobody seemed to know for sure, not even himself, maybe it was just the only pair of boots he had. And as you probably already figured out, Shirtless got his name as he never wore a shirt. He did, however, always wear a vest with his stomach sticking out since it was way too small for him, making it impossible for him to button it up. The two of them were twins and never left each other's sides. And, just as nobody knew their names, neither did anyone know their age. They looked as if they might be in their late thirties but since neither of the two were very clever and did not know their own ages nor their own names it was difficult to tell for sure.

The doors opened and the twins entered the room while dragging Kleo along with them. Her legs were scraping the wooden floorboards and her head was facing down. She slowly looked up at Matt, and as they entered, he could see that her face was completely beaten up and blood was running from her nose and forehead.

"Give it to me now, and I will let her walk away without further harm," Enzo said. This time with an even more serious look on his face.

Matt's face looked worried. He carefully and slowly reached for the parchment that was still hidden in his clothes, trying to think through what would happen once Enzo found out that a big piece was missing. He handed it over to Enzo who almost ripped it out of his hands with anger. He started to open it up and quickly saw that a piece had been ripped off.

"Where is it?" Enzo yelled from the top of his lungs; he was clearly out of patience with Matt.

"I don't know," Matt said, trying to sound confident in his voice while the tension in the room was building up.

Enzo gave a nod to one of the guards who drew a dagger from his belt and held it tightly up against Kleo's throat. She was clearly frightened and did not seem to think that the whole situation was going to end well.

"So, you expect me to believe that you don't know what happened to the parchment even though you are the only one who had it in your possession this entire time?" Enzo asked with a look on his face that Matt could not quite tell the meaning of.

Matt looked around the room and into the floor a few times trying to come up with an idea. "I burned it," he said with big worry in his voice as he looked at Kleo and saw her face turn all pale and scared.

What was to happen, he did not know, but he was definitely worried about the outcome.

Enzo's face turned red with anger as he yelled, "You burned it!" followed by a heavy sigh.

Matt stood completely still and did not make a sound.

"Escort pretty eyes outside and show her a good time," Enzo said to the twins while keeping his eyes fixed on Matt.

"No!" Matt quickly said while looking at Kleo who disappeared though the door. "You promised that you wouldn't harm her if I gave it to you."

"You brought me only one half, so I shall only keep half of my promise to you," Enzo said.

"I memorized it," Matt quickly told him while looking rather surprised with the words that had just come from his own mouth. "I memorized it," he said once more.

Enzo's facial expression made Matt nervous, and he did not know what his next move was going to be.

"Take them both and throw them into the barn. Have the men make ready, we leave tomorrow at first light," Enzo ordered, as he walked away. It was easy to tell by the way he walked off, that he was indeed both angry and frustrated.

The guards took Matt to the barn, threw him inside and locked the door behind him. He looked around but Kleo was not there. He began to kick the door trying to see if he could get it to open, and after only a few kicks, somebody from the outside unlocked the door and Matt got his fists up, ready to fight whoever it was. As the door was opened, he did not even see who was out there, as he fell over in an instant as Kleo was thrown right at him.

The door closed and was once again locked.

Kleo slowly rolled off of Matt and laid on the ground next to him. He quickly sat up and asked if she was okay however, he did not get a reply, she just looked up at him and he spotted a tear in the corner of her eye just before she quickly looked away. Matt got very quiet; he had never seen Kleo cry before. Ever since they were small kids, she had always been the tough one of the two. The worried look on Matt's face turned to anger, he wanted Enzo to pay for whatever they had done to her.

"I'm so sorry; this is all my fault," Matt whispered into her ear.

Kleo tried to get up and Matt helped her off the ground and sat by her side up against the back wall in the far end of the barn. Gently he pulled his arm around her and hugged her tightly into his body with a look on his face as if he wanted to tell her something, but he remained silent and did not speak a word.

"What exactly is it that you burned?" she asked him.

"I am not sure, but it was definitely a map, but not a regular map. It looked different. This looked more like an old treasure map, but I am not sure where it leads to. It had an island in one corner but not an island I have ever seen before, and in the other, there was a drawing of a chest decorated with gems and next to it was some sort of giant stone," Matt told her as she was falling asleep with her head on his shoulder.

He leaned his head onto hers and closed his eyes trying to get some sleep. The night went on and he was still awake trying to memorize the piece he had burned and tried his best to come up with an idea, of how, to get them out of the mess they were in.

Chapter Three

The sun was soon rising, the colors of the sky were turning brighter by the minute.

Enzo's men had made sure that everything was ready and had prepared the horses. Matt and Kleo were still asleep in the barn and had not noticed a thing in spite of the loud noises coming from outside. One of the guards pushed the door open and went inside to pour cold water from a bucket right in their faces. They both woke up in an instant, wiping the ice-cold water off with their hands. The water was so cold that they both had a shortness of breath as their bodies had gotten a great shock.

The guard kicked Matt's legs with his boot before ordering both of them to get up and hurry outside. Kleo and Matt both rushed up as it was clearly time for them to leave.

As they rushed outside, cold, and confused with what was to happen now, they quickly found themselves tied up with rope once again. This time, however, they were each placed on the back of a horse with each a guard, to make sure they did not do anything stupid or maybe even try to run off.

They started to ride out. Matt and Kleo could not really see Enzo as he was riding up in the front and they were all the way in the back. Matt continuously tried to scout for Enzo to see what was going on. He noticed Enzo had what was left of the map strapped to the saddle of his horse. The piece of the map that Enzo now had in his possession showed the way to an island where one could only assume the treasure would be held.

"We are going to the island," Matt said to Kleo while trying to keep his voice low.

Kleo did not get time to respond to him before they both were told to keep their mouth shut by one of the guards next to them.

The missing piece was only the part of the island showing the location of the treasure, which Matt strongly hoped that he had memorized correctly. For Enzo had made a promise to him, before they left, that if Matt was to fail to lead him to the treasure, or tried to double-cross him in any way, he would kill Kleo in front of his eyes using Matt's own sword.

They rode for what felt like hours on end through forests, over hills and crossed many rivers until they finally reached the shore where a ship was waiting for them.

It was an enormous ship with many beautiful decorations engraved in the wood. It had three huge white sails each with a big red cross in the middle of them. Neither Matt nor Kleo had come across anything like it before. Besides being painted in red, it looked a bit different than a regular cross. It was thinner in the middle and got wider towards all four ends.

The ship had been stolen decades ago by Enzo's grandfather and had been passed down through generations.

Enzo himself called her, *The Pride*, which obviously was not the real name of the ship, but he did tend to be a little overdramatic sometimes.

As they boarded the ship, Kleo and Matt were once again locked up. They were locked up in a cabin and the two of them had nothing better to do than to see if they were able to find anything useful in there.

Kleo had found an old dull rusted dagger on a shelf that they used to cut their hands free of the rope. Their wrists were all red and gory from the friction of the tight and dirty ropes. They desperately tried to find something they could use to rinse the wounds with so they could avoid a possible infection.

"You look there, I'll look over here," Matt said, as they both started to turn everything in the cabin inside out.

There were not many places to search in the cabin as it was quite empty. Kleo went back over to the shelves and looked through the mess of old paper and books piled up over there, while Matt searched in the drawers of an old banquette in front of the windows.

"Ha! This is our lucky day after all," Kleo said while she pulled forth an old bottle with a halfway crumbled cork and with a label on it that said 'l'eau de vie', which means the water of life. Back in the days it was only used as a medicine and was considered to, not only possess strengthening abilities, but also sanitary powers. Today most people know it as the liquor, brandy, that is being consumed all around the world.

Now Matt had heard rumors that it could be used for drinking as well as a medicine, so they had both decided to put it to the test. Matt had managed to find two small cups on a shelf and poured a modest amount in each of them. They each took a sip of the brandy, and both got disgusted looks on their faces before spitting it out on the floor. The brandy had a very poor taste which quickly made Kleo decide that it would probably be better if they just used it to clean up their wounds, for it was certainly not worth drinking. She poured a tiny bit of liquid from the bottle onto Matt's wrists and by the look on his face it was clearly uncomfortable. Kleo was next, Matt looked at her for confirmation before he washed her wrists with the liquor. The pain and stinging were intense, and Kleo nearly pulled her hands away from him as soon as it touched her.

***

A few days had already gone by on the ship, and not once had they heard from Enzo, or any of his men for that matter. They were just sailing further into the ocean and there was nothing to see in either direction but water. There was no sign of any island yet, so Matt and Kleo had plenty of time to plan their great escape and figure out when and where they would have the advantage to do so. Their loophole would be as soon as they reached the island, however, they would first need to get to the bottom of the ship and also find a way to get their weapons back.

Matt was certain that the weapons were somewhere on the ship. He swore he had seen his bow and sword attached to one of the saddles as they rode to the ship, and he had for sure also spotted the golden handle of Kleo's sword.

A storm was approaching in the horizon. Kleo went towards the windows and saw thunder and lightning were covering the sky and the waves of the sea were becoming taller than the ship. Water was starting to flush through the gaps in the windows and the ship was rocking side to side, almost shaking as if an earthquake was beneath them. Kleo and Matt knew that they needed to find some way, or something to hold onto, if they were not going to be thrown around as the ship was almost tilted sideways whenever it was hit by the tall waves. They did not have much in the room to hold onto and the small table along with a few wooden chairs were almost flying through the room as the ship was jumping over the waves nearly hitting them both while they tried to maintain their foothold.

On the top deck the crew was fighting to get the ship out of the storm in one piece. The captain was shouting out orders to the crew which could be heard all the way down to the cabin where Kleo and Matt were being tossed around.

The storm had already caused plenty of damage to the ship and one mast had cracked halfway through the center. It took two men to hold the helm steady, and five members of the crew were standing around the tall broken mast trying their best to bind it tightly together with rope, while the deck was flooded with water every two seconds causing them to be thrown around.

Enzo was inside his cabin; he was very calm and did not seem afraid or concerned about whether the ship would survive the storm or not. He did not as much as blink. Throughout the whole event he simply stood opposite his desk, not moving an inch, in spite of the ship heavily rocking side to side. While closely looking at his maps he was laying out different routes to get to the island.

Inside the other cabin, Kleo and Matt still had not found a way to secure themselves. They held on to the shelf that was built into the ship as tightly as they could trying to avoid getting hurt. Paper and books were falling from the shelf hitting them every now and then. They were both scared from not knowing if the ship would make it through the storm. Kleo grasped Matt's hand and held on to it as tight as she possibly could and closed her eyes while wishing for the storm to be over.

Not long after the storm had started to calm down along with the waves in the sea, the men on deck were slowly beginning to gain back control over the ship as well. Even though it was not completely over, the ship was steady enough for all of them to be able to keep their foothold.

Only shortly after the big storm had passed, Matt had spotted the island not too far out. He expected that they were going to reach the island at sunrise, so they had to start moving if they were to be ready in time. They assumed there would only be a few guards around on the deck at this time of night, so they would easily be able to sneak around and remain unseen. And as the night went on Kleo slowly began to pick the lock on the door, using the tip of the dagger along with a few steel tools she had found around the cabin. It did not take long before the door was opened and, slowly, they opened it up and peaked out to see if any guards were around.

Since they appeared to be all alone, they quickly snuck out and gently closed the door behind them without making a sound and walked up against the wall until they reached the stair to the deck. They could hear footsteps up there and at least two men talking. They had to be both fast and light footed if they were to reach the other side of the deck without being seen.

Being as confident as they could be they had decided to go one at a time. Kleo went first while Matt stayed hidden behind one of the barrels on deck right next to the stairs from where they came. She reached the other end with ease and Matt got ready to follow along. The guards had changed position so he could no longer see where they were. Kleo was still able to see one of the men and he was still talking to someone next to him. Kleo tried to guide Matt to the other side of the deck as she kept a close eye on him and the guards.

He was almost there but Kleo quickly gave him a sign to stop moving immediately. One of the guards must have heard a sound or spotted something in the corner of his eye, because he was now walking right towards where Matt was hiding.

Matt was getting nervous and began to breathe heavily so he covered his mouth and nose with his hand in order to stay quieter and laid down as low as he possibly could, so that the guard would hopefully not see him. The guard looked around for a minute or two but did not spot him, even though both of his feet were right in front of Matt's face. The guards went back to the other side of the deck and Matt once again had safe passage to reach Kleo. As soon as she gave him a sign to start moving, he quickly got up and rushed to her.

The easy part was now over. Now they needed to go down and reach the arsenal, get the weapons, and hide out in the panic room, that they expected to find in the lower part of the ship and stay there until the morning, where they would reach the shore and hopefully be able to escape unseen.

Matt and Kleo looked at each other and gave a small nod confirming that they were both ready to get down the stairs. They both took a deep breath before moving as neither of them knew what was waiting for them down there. If Enzo caught them trying to escape, the consequences would be far worse than they already were.

While on their toes they gently walked down the staircase at the same time trying to be as silent as possible. They got almost halfway down before one of the old wooden steps made a squeaking sound. Matt and Kleo stopped immediately and listened around if anyone had heard the sound. There were no guards in sight, so they continued down to the bottom. This time they were moving slower, going one at a time so they did not make any more noise than necessary. As they reached the bottom, they scouted the area to look for the door to the arsenal. To their surprise there were still no men around.

Kleo looked at Matt and slowly pointed towards the door to the arsenal that had caught her eye. It was right across from them on the other side of a shelf full of more old brandy bottles. They continued sneaking through the room, keeping an eye over their shoulder, should any guards approach them suddenly. They reached the door; Matt had a concerned yet wondering look on his face. How could it be so easy for them to get to the arsenal and why was there none of Enzo's men around? He looked around the room a few times making sure no one was spying on them.

Both of them entered the arsenal at the same time and the very first weapons they saw on a table, were their own. Both their swords and Matt's bow and quiver, that still held all of his arrows, were in the room. As they geared up, Kleo spotted something behind Matt. A dagger. It was a beautiful dagger with the same cross on the handle as the one they had seen on the sails of the ship. She took it with her hand and looked back at Matt and shrugged her shoulders before she attached the dagger to her boot.

After they had both geared up, they were ready to get out of there. Matt looked out of the window from inside the arsenal, they were right in front of the island now. There was no time to find the panic room beneath the ship to hide in. They needed to get to the bottom of the ship immediately and prepare to escape.

Men were heard shouting on the top deck, but from Matt and Kleo's position it was impossible to hear what was said. Had Enzo or his men noticed that they had escaped from the cabin or did they just give out orders to lower the anchor? The plan was certainly not to wait around for the answer.

Matt rushed to the window and opened it.

"We have to climb down," Matt whispered with a tense voice.

"You want to climb down the side of the ship, and then what? Swim to shore? You know I cannot swim right?" Kleo said with a wondering and concerned look on her face.

Without giving any reply, Matt was almost halfway out of the window already. Kleo sighed and followed him. It was either that or face Enzo and his crew.

The sun was yet to rise so they had the advantage of not being too visible. They moved like shadows on the side of the ship making their way down towards the water. While slowly crawling down, they both kept looking up, making sure no members of the crew were above them or getting too close to where they were. They heard some crewmembers on the deck. It sounded as if they were approaching the railing. Kleo and Matt stopped moving and tucked their bodies as close to the ship as possible, making it more difficult to spot them, should the guards decide to look down. The voices on deck were fading, making it safe for them to continue moving down. Matt stopped when they were almost halfway down. Kleo managed to climb a little further before she noticed he had stopped moving. From where she was standing, it looked as if he was searching for something, but she could not quite tell what he was up to.

"What are you doing?" Kleo whispered to him trying to understand why he had stopped.

"One second," he replied as he was looking around for something they could use as a raft in the water.

He noticed that a big wooden piece on the side of the ship appeared to be loose, maybe it had been damaged in the storm. He moved a few steps to the side in order to reach it and tried to wiggle it off with one hand. Matt knew he had to be careful not to drop it in the water since the splash would most likely draw unwanted attention from above.

It finally came loose and was quite a bit heavier than he had expected it to be. He would have dropped it if it was not for Kleo. She supported the weight with her hand from underneath and by working together they carefully got the piece of wood in the water without making any noise. Kleo got in the water first and held on tightly to the ship while Matt got himself into the water as well. He held the wood still so Kleo could safely tug one of her arms around it and get ready to swim with one arm and paddle her way to the shore with her legs. Matt was swimming next to her the entire time, helping to get her forward and making sure she was okay.

As the first sunlight appeared on the horizon, they had safely reached the shore. Matt looked back at the ship to make sure no one had followed them.

They did it. They escaped and had managed to do so unseen. Or so they tought.

Back at the ship Enzo stood in his cabin looking out the window, and he had been watching the two of them the entire time.

He had, with good reason, had a feeling all along, that the two of them would try to escape, so he had simply decided to make it easier for them to accomplish their goal. He was the one who left their weapons on the table and left the arsenal unlocked, and he was the one who made sure that they had easy passage to escape as there were no guards outside of their cabin. It had been his plan all along to help them escape and to make them believe that he was not following them.

Enzo knew from the very beginning that they would never have led him to the treasure, at least not willingly, and now all there was for him to do, was to hope that Matt truly had memorized the map, and that they would set out to find the treasure for themselves. Enzo felt like the odds were definitely in his favor, especially since they both seemed to believe that they had outsmarted him with their great escape.

"You know what to do," Enzo said to someone sitting in the shadows in the corner of his cabin.

As he stood back watching Matt and Kleo disappear into the forest, he could not help but to get a smirk on his face.

Chapter Four

"Do you even know where we are going?" Kleo said with sweat dripping from her forehead as they were making their way up a steep hill deep inside the misty forest. The forest did not look like anything they had seen before, many of the plants looked almost unreal and the majority of the flowers were definitely not like the ones they had back home. The island certainly had a different vibe, and they could both feel it, even though neither of them could quite put words on it. It was just different.

"Yes. Of course. We just need to get to the top of the forest, then we will see a mountain and on the other side of the mountain we must cross the big river, then all we need to do is to find the cave, and inside should be the treasure," he said while pointing around with his hand as if he knew exactly what they were doing before he silently said to himself, "I think."

They had walked almost all day and there seemed to be no end to the forest, and no matter how far up the hills they went it just went back down even further on the other side. Nowhere could they see a mountain, and nowhere could they see a hill big enough to get them higher than the trees. The heat from the sun and the moisture in the air had made their energy disappear fast as they had not had a single sip of water since they left the ship. They were getting sore feet from all the hiking and both Matt and Kleo had started to get blisters on their feet, caused by the friction of their shoes.

The sun was about to set, and they could feel the heat of the ground disappearing underneath them and the cold of the night was approaching fast. The warm forest was turning colder by the minute and the misty air now felt as if ice was cutting their skin and their warm breath turned visible in an instant as it merged together with the cold air.

They both started noticing that the forest had turned quieter and stopped for a second to take a closer look around, both keeping their hands close to the handles of their sword. Both Matt and Kleo were paying close attention and listening for anything moving in the shadows. There were no sounds at all, the only thing they could hear were the sounds of their own breathing. After standing there for a few seconds they decided to slowly continue ahead while staying close to one another. They only managed to take a few more steps before they both got lifted from the ground and found themselves caught in a net dangling from a tree. Neither of them could move as they were squished together so tightly inside of the trap. It was certainly a manmade trap and it seemed as if it had been there for many years since the rope that had been used to braid the net, not only looked old, but had moss growing all over it too.

Matt and Kleo were both twisting around trying to get their arms free. They were both rather uncomfortable, not only from being all tangled up, but the fact that their faces were pushed tightly up against one another made the whole thing way more awkward for both of them.

"Try reaching for the dagger in my boot," Kleo said to him as his hands were closer than her own.

His tongue was almost sticking out through the side of his mouth, almost touching Kleo's cheek, as he was struggling to reach all the way down to her boot to grab it.

"Got it!" he said and immediately began to cut through the

rope so that they could get out of there. He could not cut very fast as his hands were all twisted around from the awkward positions, they both were in, but nevertheless, he could cut.

He only needed to cut a few more pieces of rope and they would be out of there in no time. As he was cutting through the last knot, the entire net burst open and they both fell onto the ground. Matt went first with Kleo following right after. She landed on top of him and accidentally gave him a knee right in his groin.

"Sorry," Kleo said as she did feel quite bad about the knee.

"No problem," he said while struggling with the pain.

They were both aching from the fall, Matt more than her, and they slowly got back up on their feet and used a few seconds to shake off the pain since they had to get going. They were both rubbing their arms struggling to stay warm while scouting for a place to make camp. They started to collect dry wood off the ground preparing to make a fire so they could be kept warm by the flames throughout the night.

It did not take long before they found a small open spot surrounded by trees and bushes. Matt prepared the wood and started a fire, while Kleo set out trying to find something for them to eat. They were both drained with energy as they had not gotten anything to eat for days so when Kleo eventually spotted a giant bush full of blackberries, she could barely believe it. She rushed to the bush and started eating as many blackberries as she could. Plucking the berries that fast obviously caused some of the thorns to cut her hands, but she did not stop for a second to think about it. As she was filling her pockets with as many berries as possible a branch cracked loudly behind her.

Kleo stopped for a second and looked over her shoulder.

"Matt?" she whispered but did not get any response.

She heard another branch crack. This time the sound came from behind the blackberry bush.

"Matt is that you?" she asked again but still did not get any reply.

She stayed completely still as she saw a shadow moving behind her. She firmly grabbed her sword getting ready to turn around.

"What's the matter?" Matt asked and accidentally gave Kleo a huge shock.

"Have you been here the whole time?" Kleo quickly asked him with a slight relief in her voice.

"No, I just got here. I heard you calling," Matt said with a weird look on his face, clearly wondering what she was on about.

"What's going on?" he said with a slight concern.

"I thought I saw something," Kleo said while looking around, scouting for whatever was hiding in the shadows.

"Relax, probably just a snake or a rabbit. I have seen many of them around here," he said, trying to comfort her as they walked back to the camp.

As soon as they returned to the camp, both of them sat around the fire and started eating the berries that Kleo had collected. None of them said a word and silently looked into the flames while listening to the sounds coming from the forest. Wolves were howling in the distance, owls were hooting in the trees above, while the fibers in the wood could be heard creaking in the fire.

Matt had noticed that Kleo kept looking up at him as if she wanted to say something, yet she stayed silent. He looked back at her a couple of times until, to his own surprise, he opened his mouth as if he now was about to speak. She looked up at him while he just sat there with his mouth slightly open and with an odd look on his face until he just suddenly closed it again and looked back into the fire which left Kleo with a tiny, yet modest, smile in the corner of her mouth.

The awkward silence continued for a long time. It was as if they both knew what the other tried to say but neither of them had the guts to say it. The rather uncomfortable situation would have continued if they had not both been distracted by colorful lights glowing in between the trees further ahead from where they were sitting. At first Matt thought it might have been fireflies but, since the colors were not only glowing yellow but also pink and blue, they both decided to sneak over there and check it out. Kleo snuck behind some bushes and Matt hid behind the tree next to her. While they were hiding, they both noticed an unfamiliar sound, a sound unlike anything they had ever heard before, it was almost a flickering sound of wings, but mixed together with an almost magical clinging. From hearing the sound Kleo's face turned full of excitement almost as if she knew what the sound was. Matt on the other hand seemed to have no clue of what it was and just looked at her confused. She tried miming out a word to him, but he could not tell what the word was. She tried to whisper the word out to him instead, but he still could not quite make out what she was saying. Kleo rolled her eyes at Matt as she thought him to be somewhat hopeless in that particular situation and decided to whisper the word even louder in spite of her trying to stay quiet.

"Fairies," he finally heard her saying but he just shook his head as he had never heard anything more stupid come out of her mouth. Kleo apparently assumed it to be fairies, since her father had told her all kinds of stories about them when she was a little girl. She decided to walk away from the bush and approach them because there was no way she was ever going to miss her chance of seeing them for real. Matt exhaled deeply as he watched her approach, he clearly seemed to think that she was being totally reckless in that current moment, but despite that, he still decided that it would probably be for the best if he followed along with her.

He slowly came out of hiding and was met by Kleo who was standing completely still looking up into the treetops. He looked up while approaching her and dropped his jaw completely. The sight was not what he had expected, and he could barely believe his own eyes. For a minute he was certain that his eyes were deceiving him. The forest was full of fairies flying around, their wings were glowing in all sorts of different colors, they were about the size of a butterfly and had small pointy ears. Both of them were completely stunned and neither of them said a word. They had both had a gut feeling ever since they arrived on the island that something was very different, but neither of them had ever expected this.

The fairies did not seem to mind their presence in the slightest and a small group of them even began to slowly approach the two of them. They flew around their heads, possibly because they were trying to decide if they meant them any harm or came with peace.. Both Matt and Kleo had huge smiles on their faces while they enjoyed the most magical creatures being so close to them. Matt even rubbed his eyes a few times to make sure his visions were actually real and not some hallucination or a dream. One fairy flew over and sat on Matt's shoulder, his face turned rather odd from the event and Kleo could not help but laugh at him which seemed to make him almost shy. Yet another fairy approached him and was about to land on his nose and if Matt was not so ticklish and made a quick movement that scared them, the fairy would have succeeded. The fairies all flew back into the treetops and went inside small holes in the stems. Soon all the colorful lights had gone, and Kleo and Matt waited around for a few more minutes before they slowly returned to their camp.

On the way back Kleo could not stop blabbering about the fairies and was clearly excited about what they had just witnessed which Matt found quite adorable.

They had reached the camp and, as the night went on, they both laid down trying to get comfortable on the rocky ground next to the fire so they could get some sleep before they had to get moving again at first light. In between the branches, far up in the trees, there was a slight gap from where they could see the beautiful stars covering the dark night sky. They were both observing the calmness around them while trying to rest their minds. Matt closed his eyes and was slowly falling asleep but Kleo on the other hand could not find peace in her mind to get some proper rest. She stayed up for a while gazing into the starry sky.

"Matt," she said and paused herself for a second or two. "Are you awake?"

"Hmm," Matt said after a while indicating that he was listening.

"Have you thought about how we're ever getting off this island? I mean, even if we do find the treasure, we still have no way of getting home," Kleo said with a low voice while still staring into the sky. She had a troubled look on her face and patiently waited for Matt to reply.

Matt opened his eyes. He knew she was right, he had been thinking the same thing ever since they boarded the ship. How would they ever get back home?

"Unless the treasure is a flying ship of course," he said with his tired voice and with a smile hoping that it would lighten up her mood a bit. He could see her from the corner of his eye and noticed that Kleo was smiling as she closed her eyes and got ready to finally fall asleep. It was late and there was no point in worrying all night since it would not change anything anyway.

***

The sun was up. Shining through the treetops with its golden rays. The birds were singing, and the leaves were dancing in the wind. Kleo woke up from the sunlight shining into her eyes. Matt had been up for a while but could not bear to wake her up. So instead, he had been clearing the camp and gotten rid of all traces of them ever being there. It was time to go. They needed to find a way to locate the mountain as fast as possible before risking that Enzo, or his men, would get too close. Matt had been covering their tracks along the way as best as he could, making it difficult for anyone to have followed them. But one could never be too careful. As soon as Kleo had woken up they immediately set out and continued on their path from the day before.

"We need a new strategy," Kleo said as she stopped walking. "We'll never find the mountain this way, nevertheless, find out where it is wisest to go around it," she added, while looking at Matt with a look of expectation as if he would know the answer.

"You're right," Matt said while looking around for a way to get to higher ground. The trees were tall, and all the big branches were meters above the ground so there was no way he could climb them. He ran to a tree that looked stronger and taller than the others, and it had only a few thick branches all the way in the top.

"You can't climb that, there's nothing to hold onto," Kleo told him with a concerned voice as he looked like he was about to do it anyway.

Matt took off his vest and threw it on the ground. He then took off his shirt and was now standing completely shirtless in the middle of the woods. Kleo clearly enjoyed the look of his bare skin. She even zoned out for second or two as she was observing his bulky abs and strong chest muscles. Matt smiled to himself as he had noticed in the corner of his eye how she was looking at him. After realizing that she had been staring at him she got shy and turned away, acting as if nothing had happened.

"This will do," he mumbled to himself and walked closer to the tree.

He wrapped his shirt around the tree, holding a sleeve in each hand that he had also wrapped around his wrists for extra grip. He took a few deep breaths getting ready to climb the tree. Without thinking too long he took a step forward and lifted his left foot up and placed it on the tree followed by his right and up he went.

Kleo stood on the ground and could almost not bear to watch. He was almost at the top when he yelled down to Kleo.

"I can see it; it is right over there!" He pointed in the direction, but unfortunately, Kleo had no idea where the mountain was since she could not see in what direction he was pointing as she got blinded by the sun.

"Shit," he mumbled to himself as he saw that the mountain stretched from one end of the island to the other. There was no way for them to get to the other side besides climbing over which exhausted Matt even from just the thought of it.

He climbed back down and gave Kleo the bad news. She could not believe how unlucky they were all the time but since there was no way for them to get off the island their best hope was to find the treasure, or at least get to the other side of the island and get as far away from Enzo as possible. There was nothing else for them to do but continue walking, this time with a faster tempo as they were only an hour, maybe only a half, away from the mountain. Matt got dressed quickly and they set out.

Sure enough, after nearly an hour, they reached the foot of the mountain.

"At least it is shorter than I expected it to be," Kleo said optimistically while looking over at Matt who seemed to look somewhat like he was giving up.

"Yeah, it's barely a mountain, it is more like a very enormous hill that looks like it is touching the sky," Matt replied teasingly as they were about to start hiking.

Luckily the mountain was not too steep. It looked as if there was a walking path all the way up.

After they were over halfway up the mountain, Kleo kept looking back over her shoulder. She swore she heard footsteps behind them and this time she was sure that it most certainly was not Matt since he was humming and walking a few meters in front of her.

They stopped for water and took a break when they reached a brook going down the mountain. Both of them were sitting on some rocks enjoying the view and catching their breath before the quest continued but were both interrupted when they heard branches that broke behind them.

Both Matt and Kleo got up from the rocks. Matt drew his sword and went towards the sound. It came from behind some of the trees. He looked around but there was nothing to see. Kleo looked down the path from which they came to see if anything, or anyone, was there. There was nothing to see and nobody was there, there was no sign of anyone but themselves.

"Let's keep walking," Matt said while lowering his sword. He grabbed Kleo by the arm to get her moving instead of waiting around to see what had made the sound.

As they approached what appeared to be the end of the path an eagle flew right above their heads. It was not the first time they had seen this particular eagle since setting foot on the island. It had appeared a few times before and was for sure the same bird. It had easily recognizable features, like the almost golden feathers and the slightly crooked wing it had on one side, it could hardly be anything but the same eagle.

You could tell by both Matt and Kleo's faces that they were trying to figure out what was up. Were they being stalked by a random eagle, or did it just have nothing better to do than to check up on them a few times a day?

Neither of them had an answer and, before they got a chance to think further of it, they realized that the hike was almost over. They could see the top. Just as they felt relief after the long hike, a wolf jumped down in front of them and it now stood between them and the other side of the mountain.

They both grasped their swords getting ready to fight. Matt stared the wolf in the eyes and did not blink. He took a step forward and swung his sword close to the wolf hoping that it would scare it off. It did not work, it only seemed to make it angrier.

The wolf howled and walked closer to Matt showing its teeth and started growling.

Kleo was standing behind Matt getting ready to attack. She heard growling behind her and quickly turned around. Two more wolves had shown up.

"We're in trouble," Kleo said to make him look over his shoulder.

They were surrounded and was left with no choice but to fight their way out of it.

As Matt struck the first blow to the wolf opposite him, Kleo reached for the dagger in her boot and threw it at one of the wolves that jumped towards her and got ready to strike the other with her sword.

Matt struggled with the wolf that had jumped him, and caused him to drop his sword, and he now found himself in a knuckle fight that did not seem quite fair.

The wolf refused to back down, so Matt decided to take a different approach and attempted to get a grip around the wolf's neck to take it down long enough to get a hold of his sword. His plan appeared to be successful at first, but soon wolf wiggled itself loose free from his grip and took a few steps back staring him in the eyes. Matt looked for his sword, but it was yet too far out of his reach.

As the wolf tried to circle around him getting ready to jump, Matt quickly grabbed his bow and shot an arrow as fast as he could. The wolf was down in just the blink of an eye as the arrow had pierced right through its heart.

Kleo had in the meanwhile used a big stone to leap from in order to get more power and punched the wolf in the face with her knuckle which luckily disorientated it long enough for her to make a deadly strike with her sword. She looked over at the wolf that had the dagger in its side. It was still breathing so she decided to take it out of its misery.

"I really starting to hate this island," she said as she cleaned up her sword and was upset about having to kill the wolves. She knew it was either them or her but killing animals still did not come naturally to her and probably never would.

All Matt did was smile as she walked past him. He was just glad that once again they were both unharmed and he could not help but think that she was truly hardcore when it came to fighting.

She was without a doubt the better fighter of the two, which she had never failed to brag about when they were kids, but there was still no way that he would ever admit that to her of course.

Chapter Five

Back at shore Enzo's men had been building a huge camp. His plan was to claim the island as his own territory as soon as the treasure was in his hands. Many more of his ships were on their way to the island, bringing armor, food, building supplies and horses along with more men.

He was clearly preparing for more than just to settle on the island. He was preparing for battle. But a battle against who? Who was there to fight with such a great army on a lost island in the middle of the ocean?

Enzo seemed as if he was more obsessed preparing for battle than he was on pursuing Kleo and Matt, even though he was very impatient with the fact that the location of the treasure was yet to be found. He had sent a few of his men out to search the island. Not to find Kleo and Matt, but maybe they would be able to locate the treasure before them.

"Did we get any words back yet, Henry?" Enzo asked his army commander with an irritated voice.

As Henry responded with a shake of his head, Enzo got angry and hit his knuckle onto the table where his piece of the map was laid out.

Despite being his commander, Henry was in fact Enzo's uncle. As a young boy Enzo had lost his father in war and was taken in and raised by his aunt and uncle. Henry used to be the one in charge, but as he had gotten older, he had passed down the responsibility and leadership to his nephew.

Henry did not always agree with Enzo's methods and ways to get things done. Although, as his commander, and not as his uncle, he needed to respect the decisions that were made. However, that did not imply that the uncle side of him could always help himself from attempting to put some reason in Enzo's head.

"Are you sure this treasure is worth the fight?" Henry asked him with caution.

Enzo did not answer, he looked at his uncle with fury in his eyes as he walked outside. He looked around the camp and admired what they had managed to build in such a short period of time. Continuing his walk, he noticed that Shirtless and Whitefoot seemed as if they had nothing better to do than stand around talking and laughing.

"We need catapults. Catapults along the beach facing the forest," Enzo shouted towards them as he pointed at some wood laying in the sand that should be used to construct them.

The twins just stood there with a confused look on their faces. What battle were they going into? They were both clearly wondering.

"Catapults?" whispered Shirtless in a questioning manner to his brother that was standing next to him, while they both looked surprised yet very muddled.

Enzo stopped in front of the two men. Both looked frightened as they swallowed a big lump in their throats. Without saying anything he continued walking. The twins hurried over to some of the big wooden lugs and immediately prepared to start building the catapults that he had requested.

All the men were working hard, some were still building the camp, and others were preparing their armor and weapons. Some men were sitting on the edge of the forest preparing arrows for their bows and others were sharpening their swords with flints and polishing their shields.

Most of the men had a bloodthirsty look on their faces as they could not wait to get into a fight, while a few, mostly the men that were still only young boys, had a more frightened look in their eyes and seemed to fear the unknown. Many of them had never seen battle with their own eyes before. They were but orphans saved from the tough life on the streets by Enzo himself and now they were indebted to serve him.

As the night was upon them some of the last ships had finally reached the shore. All the supplies and horses had been taken off the ships and placed in the camp.

The horses were left grazing in the rim of the woods and the saddles were stored in the barn that was nearly done being built. All the swords, shields, bows and arrows had been distributed amongst the men and they were all about to put on their armor and adjust it so they would be completely prepared to ride out whenever the rest of the ships had been loaded off and as soon as the order was given to them.

They had all been given a ration of food for the night, before getting some sleep and restoring their energy for what the morning might bring.

***

Enzo was standing on the edge of the water looking deep into the dark horizon where the sun was yet to peak from behind the skies with the waves gently washing ashore touching his feet.

"I come with news, sir," Henry said as he walked up behind him.

On his shoulder sat an eagle with feathers shining like they were made of gold and in his hands, he had a small piece of wood.

On the wood it had a drawing engraved from the tip of a knife. The drawing was of the path leading to the foot of the mountain where the trail to the top was to be found.

"Get the men ready," Enzo said as his eyes were lightening up. "We ride out in an hour," he added before he withdrew to his chamber.

***

As Matt and Kleo came down over the other side of the mountain, they could finally see the river that Matt remembered from the map. They were surprised with the size of it as it was a tiny bit bigger than they had expected it to be. It was over five meters wide, and the stream was heavy, so it was most likely that it was leading to a waterfall further ahead. Matt ensured Kleo that he clearly remembered that there were not any crossing bridges on the map, and it would take too long for them to follow the river to its end, hoping to find an easier way to get across. They were running against time. Even though they had not yet seen any signs of Enzo, it would certainly be wise to assume that he would have spotted the mountain by now or at least was somewhere along the right path. Enzo might be reckless, but he was definitely not stupid.

Matt drew his sword and started chopping it into the log of a tree next to the riverbed. While he was attempting to use the blade as an axe Kleo stood on the other side ready to push the log towards the river when it slowly started to give in and tip over. The tree was finally halfway cut and started to tip over so Kleo pushed it with all the strength she had which made the tree fall in an instant.

It landed perfectly; it went across the river only touching the riverbanks without being too close to the fast-flowing water in the river.

"Now what," Kleo asked Matt hoping that he did not expect them to use the log as a bridge.

"Now we cross," Matt replied while getting ready to jump onto the fallen tree.

"I'm not walking on that," she replied while she shook her face and said, "It will never hold."

"Of course it's gonna hold. I'll go first, and you just have to follow my lead, there is nothing to be worried about," he said, trying to sound convincing as he slowly began to balance his way across the river.

Matt was almost halfway to the other side and Kleo was still on the ground hesitating to walk across. Just the thought of going out there made her palms sweaty and her knees feel weak, almost shaking, as if they were going to collapse as soon as she took a step forward. He had finally reached the other side and jumped down onto the ground.

It would not be long before the sun would start to set and disappear behind the mountain, so their ability to see clearly would only go down from here.

"Come on, it's easy," Matt shouted to her from the other side of the river.

She placed her foot onto the log, grabbed it with both of her hands and lifted herself up. She took a few deep breaths and started to walk carefully. After reaching almost halfway across, the tree started to give in. She looked over at Matt completely frozen and scared. He was clearly worried, but he knew he could not show her as it would just make her more nervous than she already was.

"Just keep going. You can do it," he said which made her take a few more steps towards him.

When she got further the tree began to shake and the middle of it sunk down towards the river. The log was about to crack.

"I promise, everything is going to be fine." That was the last words that came out of his mouth right before the log split in two.

And with a blink of an eye Kleo was gone. She was under the water getting pushed down from the heavy current.

Matt ran as fast as he could next to the river trying to spot her. He called out for her as loud as he could, but she was nowhere to be seen. Further down her head emerged from the water a few times long enough for her to take a few breaths. She was fighting with all she had to stay on top of the water. He ran as fast as he could trying to get in front of her so he would be able to get her out of the water. She was pulled back towards the riverbank from which they came. Matt had gotten way ahead of where he last saw her head pop up and got ready to drag her out from the water.

Kleo was fighting. Almost being out of air, she had no idea in what direction Matt was nor did she have any orientation under the water as to where she was. As she was pushed closer to the edge, she was close to hitting her head on the rocks a few times. Fortunately, she was grabbed by her hand just as she was about to pass out. She got dragged out of the water and was laid on the ground and started coughing up all the water she had in her lungs.

"Leave her alone," Matt yelled as loud as he could from the other side of the river. He was aiming with his bow and was ready to take a shot.

Kleo looked at Matt on the other side of the river. It took her a few seconds to realize that he was not the one who had pulled her out of the water. As she looked up, she was shocked to see who had saved her from nearly drowning and could barely believe her own eyes. A very handsome young man was standing right next to her. A man she had never seen before, and he did not look like any of Enzo's guards so who was he, and where did he come from?

The young man looked over at Matt while he lifted his hands in the air trying to show that he meant them no harm.

"Are you all right?" Matt shouted to Kleo. He was clearly worried about her, but he did not want to take his eyes off the man next to her.

She nodded back to him and slowly wiped some of the water off her face.

"Get away from her," Matt shouted while keeping his aim on him.

"Matt, relax," Kleo said while giving him a sign with her hand for him to lower his bow.

"I was just trying to help," said the young man while slowly lowering his hands back down and took a step aside from her.

When Kleo slowly got back on her feet, the young man offered to give her a hand. She took his hand and he gently helped her get off the ground and made sure she was okay which certainly seemed to irritate Matt who was stranded on the other side.

"You know there's a bridge further down that crosses the river right?" he asked while giving Matt a sassy look from across the river.

Kleo could not believe it. A bridge. All this fuss when there had been a safe way for them to get across this entire time. Matt looked surprised and slightly embarrassed. He had sworn that the map did not show a bridge. Maybe the young man was lying or maybe someone had set foot on the island after the map was made and had built the bridge.

"Show us," Matt said as he started walking in the direction where a bridge supposedly was.

"My name is Hunter by the way," he said to Kleo while taking forth his hand to formally greet her.

"I'm Kleo. Thank you for the help before," she said as she shook his hand while looking rather ashamed.

Matt rolled his eyes from the other side of the river. How did she not find it strange that a man just happened to be out there exactly in the same place as they were and just happened to be there in time to save her? They had walked for about half an hour, without anyone saying much, before they reached the bridge that Hunter had told them about. The bridge was wide and steady enough for at least ten grown men to cross at the same time. Kleo and Hunter crossed the bridge to reach Matt on the other side. Hunter put forth his hand in order to greet Matt in a friendly way, however, he ignored him and went straight over to Kleo, checking if she was injured in any way. Besides her body being a little sore and her clothes being all soaked, she was fine. Kleo offered Hunter to tag along with them for a while, which did not seem to please Matt in the slightest as he had a strong gut feeling that something about him simply did not seem right.

As they were walking Kleo started to feel a lot of pain in her side making it hard for her to walk. The last thing she wanted was for Matt to worry even more, so she kept quiet and tried to bite though the pain as best as she could. The pain gradually became worse the further they walked and soon she almost collapsed as her legs could not carry her any longer. Matt rushed to support her and asked what was wrong, but she was almost passed out.

"Help me get her over there," Matt ordered Hunter and pointed towards a spot a little off from the main path.

They each grabbed one of her arms and slowly guided her towards a place where she could lay and rest. Matt noticed she kept her hand on her waist. He slowly lifted up her shirt and saw her entire waist and ribs were bruised. She had most likely hit something in the water.

"She'll be fine; she just needs some rest," Matt said while clearly being worried about her.

He was getting ready to set up camp for the night and make a fire. Hunter was helping collecting the firewood while Kleo was resting.

"I didn't ask for your help," Matt said.

"I know," Hunter said, while he continued to collect the wood.

Matt could not help but wonder what this guy was up to. How had he even let Kleo convince him to let that guy stick around?

He had so many unanswered questions in his head, but one thing was for sure, Hunter had a long way to go if he was trying to earn his trust.

***

All three of them were laying around the fire keeping warm throughout the night. Kleo and Hunter were both sleeping, while Matt stayed awake. He wanted to keep a close eye on Hunter in case he was truly up to no good but as the night went on it became harder for him to stay awake, and he was struggling to keep his eyes open. His eyes were constantly closing and within a few seconds he too was asleep. He only managed to sleep for a few minutes before something moved through the bushes causing Matt to wake up. He grabbed the handle of his sword getting ready to face whatever was approaching. It was just Hunter returning to the camp.

"I didn't mean to wake you, I just had to go uhm... nature called," he said before he laid back down on the ground to go back to sleep. Matt looked at him for a few seconds before he closed his eyes too. However, this time he kept his sword in his hand as he knew something was not right. Only a few moments later Hunter opened his eyes back up and lifted his head a bit to look over at Kleo. She was still sleeping and had not noticed a thing. Hunter got a smile on his face while he was watching her in her peaceful sleep. But for some reason the smile quickly turned into a rather unhappy face almost as if he was overthinking something. After observing her for a short while he laid back down and slowly fell sleep.

Chapter Six

The next morning Hunter was woken up from his sleep by Matt and Kleo who were having an argument just outside of the camp. He could not hear much of what they were saying but they were definitely arguing about whether or not they could trust him. Kleo did not care what Matt thought about him, it would only be fair to give him a chance, since he did after all save her life. Matt needed more convincing as he still felt certain that Hunter had been the one who had been following them the entire time.

"Stop fraternizing with the enemy," Matt said to her with a somewhat frustrated tone of voice.

"The enemy?" Kleo said and was clearly chocked about his way of approaching the matter.

"I just mean, don't trust him too much," he said.

"Thanks for the warning but I'll decide for myself who to trust," Kleo said and left the conversation since she had had enough of his mistrust in everybody all the time.

Hunter got up and grabbed his gear. He was about to walk over to them in order to say his goodbyes.

"I am happy to see you are doing better," he said to Kleo with a gentle smile. "I will be going now." He clearly did not mean for them to get upset about his presence or cause any trouble.

"You're staying with us," Matt said as he had decided by himself that he still did not want to let Hunter out of his sight.

"Okay," Hunter said confused while looking at Kleo who

looked equally as surprised with the words that had just come out of Matt's mouth. Matt started walking. He did not want to waste any more time because of some punk who thought he was being clever.

***

After they had been walking for a few hours, Matt turned around to ask Hunter why he had even been wandering around an uninhabited island alone while deeply implying that he knew something was off about him.

"I was part of the crew on a ship that sank a few weeks ago. I passed out in the water and when I woke up, I found myself here on the island. None of the other crewmembers survived, or at least I did not find any of them yet. I only found you guys wandering around. So how about you explain to me what you are doing here yourselves?" Hunter said while looking at Matt with an intense look in his eyes.

"We're here to find something," Kleo said as she tried to interrupt the staring contest the guys were having with one another.

"What is it that you need to find?" Hunter curiously asked.

"A cave. So, have you happened to find one of those as well?" Matt asked with a heavy referral to the bridge from the day before.

"No, unfortunately I haven't, but I'll let you know if I find one. Why exactly is it that you need to find a cave?" Hunter said while looking at Kleo.

"If the myth is true, a golden chest is said to be found inside the cave. And we need to find it before someone else does," Kleo told him before Matt tried to shut her up from giving away too much information.

"I've heard about it," Hunter said as he looked back and forth at both of them while telling them about a myth. "I've heard that in spite of the treasure only consisting of one single chest, it is said that the value inside is far greater than any amount of gold possible for even a horse to carry and that the treasure has been lost and forgotten about for centuries."

"How do you know all this?" Matt asked with a suspicious look on his face.

"My father has always been very interested in old myths and obsessed with stories about great treasures," he replied while looking into the ground.

If what he was saying was true, and he knew about it, who else might know? And if Enzo got to the treasure before them, he would become the most powerful man and he would take over their land with the blink of an eye. They could not let that happen. It was a lot to take in for them both and since they were all tired, they had decided to rest their legs for a bit before they had to move on. Hunter went out to see if he could find something for them to eat while Kleo and Matt stayed behind.

"He's been gone for quite some time now," Kleo said while looking out to see if she could spot Hunter.

"Good," Matt replied while drawing in the dirt with a stick. Clearly, he could not seem to care less about him.

"Why do you have to be so mean to him? He's just trying to help us out," Kleo said since she truly did not understand why Matt made such a big issue about him.

"I just don't like him, and I still don't trust him," Matt said while shrugging his shoulder.

"You could at least give him a chance; he did after all save my life, remember?" Kleo said to him while looking deep into his eyes.

Matt looked up at her. She was waiting for him to say something, but no words came out of his mouth. Kleo got upset with Matt's inability to respond so she stood up and went out to check on Hunter. Matt stayed behind and stared back into the ground. From the look on his face, it was clear that he still blamed himself for the fact that she almost drowned and he deeply wished that he had been the one who had been able to save her.

Kleo did not get far before Hunter came walking back with two dead birds in his hand.

"How did you manage to catch those?" Kleo asked surprised.

"They do not call me Hunter for nothing," he said with a big proud smile on his face as he went over to Matt who was getting a fire started.

Hunter nearly threw the two dead birds in Matt's face which did in fact seem to be slightly on purpose.

"Good job," Matt said in a rather cocky manner.

"Oh, so you think you can do better than that?" Hunter said.

"Yes," Matt said and walked away.

Kleo sat next to Matt while he was preparing the food, she noticed that Hunter was carving in a piece of wood with his dagger while sitting by himself on a rock.

"What do you suppose he's making?" she asked Matt.

"I don't know, why don't you just go over there and ask him?" Matt said while not seeming to care much about it.

"Why are you being like that?" Kleo said.

Matt did not reply and just continued preparing the food.

"How are you feeling?" he asked her all of a sudden while looking at the spot where the bruises on her body were.

"Oh, it's fine," Kleo said trying to not make Matt worry too much about her. It was still bad and hurt a lot whenever she was moving but it did not matter to her. They had something more important to worry about, which was to locate the treasure before Enzo found it.

"You should go see if you can find some fruit around here, so that you'll have something to eat," Matt said to her.

All they had were the birds Hunter had killed and Matt knew Kleo well enough to know that she was not going to eat them, no matter how hungry she might be. She got up to look for more berries around the forest while staying close to the camp. Matt was so busy cooking the food that he had not even noticed that Hunter had gone after her.

"You shouldn't walk around here by yourself," Hunter said which startled Kleo since she clearly seemed to believe that no one was around.

"You scared me," she said while continuing to look around for food.

"What are you looking for?" he asked curiously.

"I thought I saw some berries around here when we arrived," she said while pointing around in the area she believed them to be around.

Hunter just stood there awkwardly and looked at her feeling misplaced which was quite understandable considering the circumstances.

"I'm sorry about Matt, he is not usually like this," she said.

"It's no problem, I guess he feels intimidated by me being here," Hunter said.

"Why would he be intimidated by you?" she said.

"Oh, I don't know," Hunter said and smiled to himself.

Kleo continued to look for berries but did not have any luck. Hunter tried to look as well, but it was clear to see that he did not have a clue what he was doing and sort of just mimicked whatever she was doing, which of course had caught her attention.

"How long have you two been together?" Hunter asked.

"Together? No, we're not together," Kleo said while blushing.

"Sorry, I thought you were. I can tell he cares much about you," Hunter said before turning around to walk back to the camp.

Kleo tried to get the goofy smile on her face to go away, along with her blushed cheeks, before she returned to the camp because she did not want Matt to see it or ask questions.

The food had been prepared and all three of them gathered around the fire to enjoy some food before it was time to get on the move again. They all sat there quietly not speaking a word to one another. Kleo eagerly tried to give a sign to Matt to have him say something, but he ignored her. She looked at Hunter, but he was just looking up in the sky while eating the wings of one of the birds. The awkward silence continued. It was hopeless, Kleo thought to herself. Everything would be much easier if they could just get along, or at least if they would just try.

As soon as they were all done eating it was time to put out the fire, remove all trace of themselves and continue on their path. Matt was burying the last of the ashes when they heard someone in the forest close by. It sounded like two men talking. Matt looked up at Kleo who was desperately looking side to side. She was looking for Hunter, but he was nowhere around. He was gone. Matt tried to listen closer to see if it might be Hunter who was talking to someone. But who would he be able to talk to out here and why would he walk away without saying anything?

Kleo and Matt snuck out in between the trees trying to get

closer to the voices. They could hear that whoever was talking, was walking straight towards them so hopefully they would soon be able to see who it was. Both of them tried to stay completely quiet to make sure they would not expose themselves. Matt was ready with his sword in case it might not go their way. Two men were approaching and from what they were wearing it would only be wise to assume that they were some of Enzo's men. The two men made their way through the forest and seemed to not pay much attention to the surroundings, nor did they seem to be looking for anything. They were just passing through. Matt surely believed that Enzo had sent them out to either find the treasure or they had been sent to find him and Kleo. He turned around to see if Hunter had appeared, but he was still nowhere around.

Matt got startled by a loud sound of something that snapped, which came from a branch underneath his own foot. Kleo looked at the men who luckily did not seem to have noticed. Only moments later the two men stopped almost in front of Matt and Kleo, maybe they had heard them after all. Kleo looked at Matt in order to find out what they should do next. Matt was debating with himself whether they should back away or get rid of the men for good. Before he had a chance to conclude anything Hunter jumped out of nowhere and knocked out one of the guards with a wooden log and, just as the other man turned around, he threw a punch in his face causing him to fall to the ground and land right beside the other. Hunter brushed off his hands as if it had been a piece of cake to take out the two men, and to be fair, even Matt was impressed with his ease.

"Where've you been?" Kleo asked while both her and Matt walked out from their hiding spot.

Hunter looked surprised to see that they were even there and nervously looked down at the two men he had just knocked out.

"Uhm... I heard voices, so I went to check it out," he said.

"You should have let us know," Matt said rather angry.

"Maybe you would have needed help," Kleo added.

"Well, I didn't," Hunter said and started walking.

Matt and Kleo just looked at each other and both decided to not waste more time on talking and just get on with it.

"Hurry up, they might wake up soon, so we have to get out of here," Hunter said to get them both to move faster.

Matt did not seem happy with how Hunter had taken charge and wanted to say something to him. Kleo knew Matt too well, she could smell from a mile away that he wanted to confront Hunter, so she took his hand trying to make him calm down and just leave it this once. The touch of Kleo's hand shocked Matt at first since he did not expect it at all, but he said nothing and chose to just enjoy the moment and did his best to ignore Hunter who was too busy walking ahead of them which was in fact a quite odd thing to do since he did not know the way.

***

Horses were galloping down the trail in great haste and the sound of heavy footsteps could be heard from miles away in spite of the loud noise coming from splashing water in the heavy current whenever it hit against the rocks in the river. Enzo and his men had almost reached the bridge thanks to the extra wooden piece they had received from the eagle. They were no more than a few hours' ride behind Kleo and the others. Enzo knew they were gaining on them, and you could tell by the look in his eyes, that had turned more bloodthirsty and intense, that it was clear that he had become far more eager to get his hands on the treasure the closer they got.

"Sir, the men are tired, the horses are exhausted, and we could all use some water. We should rest," Henry said cautiously to Enzo.

"Rest?" Enzo said back as if he had no clue what that word even meant.

He slowed down the pace and looked back at his men. They did indeed look tired, nevertheless, Enzo did not seem happy with the thought of stopping. In the far back he could see Whitefoot and Shirtless almost asleep and even about to fall off their horses a time or two.

"They can get ten minutes," Enzo said to Henry. "Have them water their horses in the meantime," he then shouted to Henry who was about to make his way down to the men.

As Henry approached the men, he had a very sad look on his face. Even though he was Enzo's uncle he did seem to have his doubts as to whether or not Enzo actually trusted him, or if he could in fact trust his own nephew himself. Not that anything in particular had happened to cause the doubts in Henry's mind, but it was Enzo's never-ending lust for power that over the years seemed to have manipulated his mind, making him more selfish and careless than he used to be. Back in the days Enzo would have done anything for his men and always made sure that they had everything they needed. Now he did not even care much for if they had eaten or even rested. He used to see his men as equals, now they were nothing but his own personal puppets. It was clear that Henry feared that the power within the treasure that they had set out to find would only worsen Enzo's intentions and heighten his lack of sympathy even further.

***

The trail they were following became more and more narrow. There were no longer any green trees around and the whole forest looked like it had burned down years ago. Ashes flew around the air like snow falling from the sky. While walking through the dead forest hissing noises kept sounding from the bushes.

"Snakes," Hunter whispered as he pointed to his ear having the others be aware of the sounds.

Before he even took his hand back down a snake jumped up out of nowhere and tried to bite Matt. The snake had a bright blue body and both the tail and head were orange. The snake would have succeeded if Kleo had not been quick to draw her sword and cut the snake's head off right before it managed to bite him.

"Thank you," Matt said to her while still in shock.

"Keep an eye out for more," Hunter said in the background just before another snake jumped out of the dead bushes.

This time it went straight for Hunter. Thankfully he was prepared, and he had slain the snake before it got too close. All three of them carefully proceeded while keeping their swords ready in case of any more surprises jumping towards them.

"Nice sword by the way," Hunter said to Matt. "I've never seen one with a black blade before."

"Thanks," Matt said, trying to sound very smug.

"Where did you get it from?" Hunter asked, being curious as he was.

"I borrowed it," Matt replied while attaching the sword to his belt.

"Borrowed it?" Hunter sassily asked.

Matt did not say anything and tried to ignore Hunter's comment.

"You mean you stole it?" Hunter said and gave Matt a look as if he was sure that Matt was lying to him.

"No, I mean I borrowed it," Matt replied. This time you

could tell by the sound of his voice that he was getting rather annoyed by Hunter's questions.

"I don't mind, I've stolen a great deal of things myself when I was your age," Hunter said in an attempt to be funny while provoking Matt a little. He was only a few years older than him, but the fact that he was both taller, and older, definitely seemed to bother him without a doubt.

Matt was about to snap at Hunter, and he would have done so if Kleo had not given a sign for them to stand still and keep quiet. They had gotten further through the dead woods and the hissing noises had disappeared completely. Not only had the hissing stopped, but all sounds of the forest were gone. No snakes, no birds, no wind. It was a little too quiet, making them all uncomfortable and nervous of what might lie ahead. It had to be something bad if even the snakes feared it. They stopped moving as they heard something approaching, the sound came from all around them, and yet they had no vision of what was making the sound. Standing with their backs against each other ready to fight, a loud howl appeared to come from right in front of them.

"Great. More wolves," Matt said with distress as he could not believe that he had to fight them once more.

The howling continued, though this time it came from more than one wolf. It sounded as if a big pack of wolves were approaching. Maybe ten or twenty were close by.

"Run," Hunter said as he saw the wolfpack running towards them in the distance. There were at least fifteen of them and it would not be wise for them to try and fight them.

They ran through the forest as fast as their legs could possibly carry them. They left the path and ran into the crowded trees and bushes hoping it would make them less visible. Kleo as the stronger runner was in the front with Matt and Hunter a few feet behind her. The wolves were gaining on them and one wolf was now running right next to Hunter while the rest of the pack were a little further behind. The wolf ran closer and pushed Hunter. He almost fell to the ground but luckily Matt supported him making sure he stayed up on his feet.

Hunter cut the wolf's leg with his sword, causing it to fall behind only a bit. The ground became more rough and uneven making it harder for them to run fast, so they changed direction back out to the trail, but soon the path disappeared completely, turning into nothing but a giant thornbush. It was completely dead, the twigs were nearly black, and the rest of the bush was grey, some of it had turned to ashes already while the rest remained. They turned around getting ready to face the wolves who suddenly had stopped. One of the wolves was sniffing the air while the rest of the pack were having rather anxious behavior. The entire wolfpack looked scared as if they were fearing something nearby. A wolf turned around and started running away and it did not take long before the rest of the pack followed suit.

"That's right, run away you cowards," Hunter said while waving his sword around.

"I wonder what got them so scared?" Matt said to Kleo who was for some reason facing the other way.

"Kleo," he said trying to get her attention.

"Do you smell it?" she said to them, who both seemed to have no idea of what she meant.

The smell of the air had changed, and it also seemed to be denser. It almost had the smell of fresh smoke, or the smell that comes from burning wood when the fire is about to go out, all mixed together with the smell of a moist dungeon or maybe a swamp.

The cave had to be nearby.

Since the wolves were long gone back the way they came from, the three of them had decided to spread out and search for the entrance as it would hopefully be much faster. Matt was clearly not fond of the idea, as it meant that Hunter would be able to roam around freely out of his sight, but he did agree with the fact that they were able to cover more ground in a shorter period of time if they split up. Kleo went towards the left following the edge of the trees that led her to a meadow. It was shining with light and the colors from all the different flowers made everything seem even brighter. But there was no sign of the entrance to the cave.

Hunter had gone to the right. He did not get far before he had spotted some footprints from a pack of wolves. It could not have been from the wolves they just ran from. These prints looked old. Now he was aware that wolves usually liked to spend some time in caves, and they were also quite good at locating them so he decided to track the prints to see where they might lead.

Matt had made his way straight through the bushes, cutting his way through them using his sword. A few of the thorns had scratched his arms and ripped a hole in his shirt. It was a dead end. As he reached the other side of the bushes all there was to see was rocks. Rocks on top of rocks, leading to a small edge facing a lake. He was debating with himself whether or not he should climb down to see if the entrance was somewhere down there, fortunately, he got interrupted just as he was about to start his climb. He had been interrupted by Hunter who was calling out for him and Kleo.

Matt and Kleo, who had heard his shouting as well, had both rushed back to where they had last seen Hunter, but he was nowhere in sight. They called out for him trying to locate where his voice came from. Hunter called for them again and they both rushed towards the sound. When they passed the footprints that

Hunter had been following, they both drew their swords as they did not know if he might have called for them in need of help. Maybe he found the wolfpack and not the entrance to the cave. They finally reached him and saw that he was not in any danger, or at least there were no wolves around. The only thing to be spotted, besides Hunter, was a giant entrance to a cave.

They had found it. Finally.

All three of them stood side by side as they admired the entrance. It was magnificent. Fully decorated with ancient drawings carved in the stones surrounding it and bright blue and purple flowers were covering the grounds. It was absolutely the most intriguing and beautiful sight any of them had ever seen.

As they were about to enter the cave, they all took a few deep breaths gathering their courage to walk inside. It would be unwise to let themselves be fooled by the beauty and assume that where they were about to set foot would be as lovely a sight on the inside as it was on the outside, since none of them had any idea about what was waiting for them once they entered.

Neither of them seemed to have paid any attention or given the drawings any thought as they walked right past them without taking a closer look. The drawings and symbols told a story, a story about the cave and what was to be found in its great abyss. Even though it was hard to make out what all the symbols meant some of them were quite clear. It appeared to be the story of knights carrying the chest to the cave where they built traps and riddles in order to keep it safe. There was a cross, the same as the one on the sails of the ship they had arrived with, and the dagger Kleo had found, next to the drawing of the knights. In the end there was a drawing of the chest again, this time opened, and next to it was what looked like an oval stone of some kind.

Chapter Seven

They had walked into the cave; it was lighted up from the sunshine shooting in from outside. Pillars were formed from stone and the ground was full of small cave-pools that had the most beautiful turquoise colors and the flowers, like the ones they had seen before entering the cave, were sprouting around them.

It was absolutely beautiful.

As they got further in, the sunlight could no longer reach the depths of the cave and the flowers no longer grew beneath their feet.

It got darker, neither of them had clear enough vision to see what was surrounding them or where they were walking. The smell of fresh flowers had disappeared, and a foul smell emerged from the deep corners of the cave. Water could be heard dripping down from the sides of the walls causing echoes to be heard in the deep. The floor was covered in water making splashing sounds whenever they took a step forward and wingbeats from bats were heard all around them as they reached deeper inside the cave.

Matt hit what felt like a wooden branch with his foot. He picked it up and tore a piece of his shirt off so that he could use it to wrap around the end of the branch and make a torch and he had asked the others to look around to see if they could feel or see anything that he could use to light it on fire. The bats had been disturbed by their presence and had started to fly around. All three of them were waving around with their arms trying to scare away the bats who were flying around their heads at high speed. Neither of them could actually see the bats but they could feel the wind from their wings whenever they passed them by.

Hunter had found a slightly damp stone and handed it to Matt. He tried for a while to make a spark but no matter what he did it simply did not work, Hunter took over and gave it all he could, hoping that he could make a spark appear, but no, nothing worked. It was impossible, and the flying bats did not necessarily make it easier for them to concentrate on what they were doing.

They both gave up and Matt asked if Kleo might want to give it a try. She did not respond, and they both turned around only to realize that she was not even there. How could she just vanish without them knowing?

"Kleo. Kleo where are you?" Hunter said while squinting his eyes hoping that he would be able to see better into the darkness.

Matt shushed him as he heard footsteps coming towards them from deeper inside the cave. This time there was no way it could be Hunter following them. While they both stood completely still holding their breaths trying to be as quiet as possible, Kleo walked up behind them.

"Here you go," she said while handing Matt a flint. You could tell by the look on her face that she was wondering what on earth they both were doing. It looked like they had seen a ghost or something.

"Where were you?" Matt asked with a relieved voice when he saw that nothing had happened to her.

She had simply found her way back out of the cave as she remembered spotting a bunch of stones in front of the entrance that were perfect for lighting up a torch.

Matt sighed and shook his head. It appeared that both the guys had just been so focused on getting the torch lit that they did not notice her walking away. Hunter kept looking into the cave. Was there someone else inside the cave walking around spying on them, or was the sound of footsteps just echoes from Kleo walking back inside that they had heard? Finally, the torch was lit, and they were able to look around. The whole cave was packed with bones from dead animals and the piece of wood that Matt thought he had used to wrap his cloth around appeared to be a large brittle bone from a dead animal. A wolf perhaps, judging by the size of it. His face looked rather unsatisfied holding the bone in his hand while Hunter chuckled in the background just seeming to be finding the situation rather amusing to observe.

"It looks as if they were recently killed," Hunter said and pointed towards a dead wolf laying on the floor next to her cubs.

"What do you suppose killed them in here?" Kleo asked him.

"I don't know, a bear perhaps?" he answered.

"Great, keep an eye out for anything moving, especially bears," Matt said while they all continued to walk further inside the cave.

From the torch being lit they were finally able to see where they were going. The cave was larger than they had expected and there was no way for them to see the end of it. Further ahead of them the walls were covered in drawings, like they had seen at the entrance.

"See, that one right there matches your dagger," Hunter said to Kleo while pointing to the wall at a cross.

"There is the chest like the one on the map," Matt said and pointed to a drawing of a chest.

"What do you think that means?" Kleo asked while pointing to a drawing with two knights lifting an oval stone above their heads.

None of them answered as they had no idea what a stone had to do with the treasure. Confused as they were, they all had the same pondering looks on their faces trying to make out what any of it meant.

"Look at th…" Kleo did not get to finish her sentence as she was interrupted by a whining not too far behind her.

She turned around trying to spot where the sound had come from.

"Did you guys hear that?" she asked them while already being halfway to some stalagmites to see what might be hiding behind them.

"Be careful," Matt said while staying alongside of Hunter, next to the wall with the drawings.

Kleo looked back at Matt with a feisty face while she continued walking towards the sound. What could possibly be so dangerous that it was both hiding and whining at the same time? she thought.

As she approached, the whining had stopped.

Before peeking behind the stones to see what was there, she had drawn her sword and was prepared just in case something bad was hiding behind there.

"Oh, my god," Kleo whispered to herself in shock.

She slowly squatted down and gently placed her sword on the ground trying not to make any sudden movements.

"What is it?" Hunter said in the background.

Kleo took her index finger and placed it on her mouth giving the guys a sign to stay quiet.

The guys were once again left confused. They could not see what was behind there, they only saw Kleo reaching her hands out for something.

"It's okay, don't be scared," she said while slowly getting

back up. In her arms she held a cub. Not just any cub, this was a little wolf. Matt and Hunter both looked equally startled as they saw the creature she had in her arms. It was rather big, certainly not a newborn, it was at least a few months old, maybe three.

"He's injured," Kleo said as she had spotted an open wound on its side.

"What do you plan on doing with him then?" Hunter asked her.

"The wound is not that bad; it'll heal by itself. But we cannot leave him here," she said and looked up at Matt trying to convince him that they had to bring the wolf along with them.

"No," he said. "I don't want an angry wolf mom on my tail because you want to have a pet. Besides, as soon as he grows big, he will be an even bigger problem."

"You don't suppose that the wolf lying dead further behind us with the cubs were his family?" she asked him. "The cubs were about the same size as him. I don't think he has anyone."

Matt looked at the cub who was looking at him with its goofy fluffy face and big eyes.

"Let's keep moving," he said while giving Kleo a nod since he realized that she would not give up the fight about bringing the wolf along.

She slowly placed the cub on the ground and gave him a few pets. The wolf was enjoying every moment, so much that he almost lost his balance from leaning towards the strokes coming from Kleo's hands. The minute Kleo got back up and started walking the wolf followed her straight away. She nearly left without her sword but remembered it at the last second and rushed back to pick it up.

Crystals were starting to form in the rocks and were glittering through the cave as they were sticking out through cracks and gaps all around them. Purple, blue, and green colors were shining around them as they continued walking through the cave. All three of them were completely mesmerized with what they were seeing. It almost looked as if the shiny night sky was flickering all around them whenever the light coming from the torch reflected on the crystals. The wolf ran a little ahead of the others but kept looking back to make sure that Kleo had not left his sight. Matt shook his head when he noticed that Hunter barely could not keep his eyes off of the crystals. He was clearly intrigued by them. Matt on the other hand seemed more fascinated by Kleo and had a hard time not gazing on her when the lights from the crystals made her glow up even more than he already thought she did. She started feeling the pain from her injury again and this time it felt as if the pain became worse with every single step she took. Her face had tuned pale and drops of sweat had started to form on her forehead. Matt quickly noticed that something was not right and walked closer to her to check out what was going on.

"Are you all right?" Matt asked her while laying a hand on her shoulder.

All she did was look at him trying to smile through the pain so that he would not worry but she had a hard time getting any words out. Matt obviously noticed her strange behavior and knew that she was trying to cover up something. He stopped walking for a few seconds letting her get a little further ahead as he was trying to figure out what was going on.

In the meantime, Hunter had been examining the crystals. He clearly could not help himself; he went over to one of the purple crystals and tried to make it come loose from the wall. It was fastened too well so he took his dagger and attempted to cut it out instead.

"Leave it," Matt said. He certainly did not want to wait around for Hunter.

All Hunter did was nod, pretending that he was on his way. Kleo was walking up front alongside of the cub and Matt was right behind them. Hunter was in the back still decided to get the crystal loose from the wall. Pearls of sweat were running down his forehead from the struggle and his cheeks had turned red. Even though he had realized that he was probably not going to bring home a crystal, he still could not help himself but to try at least one more time. He got a better grip on his knife and this time he really tried to shove it as far inside the gap as possible. As soon as the dagger got inside the wall the ground started shaking beneath their feet.

Matt and Kleo stopped moving and looked back at Hunter to see what was happening.

"What did you do?" Matt shouted to Hunter with anger.

The cub ran off further into the cave and got away just before big spiky stones began to fall down around them. Matt grabbed Kleo and pushed her up against the wall making sure she would not get hit. Hunter jumped to the side and was almost hit by one of the rocks that landed right next to his feet. While the stones continued to fall down around them, Kleo and Matt were staring right into each other's eyes and were so close that they could even feel the heat coming from the other's skin. The shaking stopped and no more stones were coming down. Hunter took a step forward and brushed dust off his sleeves and continued walking as if nothing had happened. Matt slowly stepped away from Kleo while looking at her with a look on his face as if he yet again wanted to say something. She could tell by the look on his face that he felt awkward, and she could not blame him because she felt exactly the same way.

"Are you ready to get moving?" Hunter said while wondering why both of them were acting so strangely.

Matt started walking and bumped his shoulder into Hunter's

as he passed him.

***

Enzo and his men had reached the end of the path.

"Where do we go now?" Henry asked him.

"Look for signs," Enzo said as he got off his horse.

All his men were carefully looking around for leads to guide them in the right direction. Some footprints were still visible on the ground, however, they went in many different directions. A few of the men split up in groups, each tracking to see where the footprints would lead to. Dark rainclouds started to form in the sky and pouring rain followed. It was becoming dark making it more difficult to see. The footprints were about to be washed away so they needed to hurry up if they wanted to find the right direction leading to the location of the treasure.

"Over here," a guard yelled. He had followed prints leading him to the right.

Enzo hurried over to see what the guard had found. He pushed his men aside as they were in his way.

"Move!" he yelled at them as he tried to make way for himself.

A piece of ripped fabric had been tied around the twigs on one of the many bushes next to them. Enzo got a smile on his face.

"We set camp here for tonight," he said as he walked towards Henry holding the fabric in his hands.

"What is it?" Henry curiously asked him.

"It is our heading," he replied while he looked in the direction of the path they had to follow while it was slowly covered with the water pouring from the sky above them.

Chapter Eight

They had walked around the tunnel all night without even realizing and neither of them seemed to notice how exhausted and tired they really were as they had been deeply focused on completing their quest.
The structure of the cave was changing. The crooked walls had flattened out, the surface was smooth and almost had a shiny look to it. There was no longer any sound of dripping water and the air felt less thick. In the end of the cave there was a great opening leading them into what seemed to be a great hall.

All around the room there were torches hanging on the walls, Kleo quickly took the torch from Matt's hand and used it to light the others. The hall they were standing in was beautifully decorated all around, and it had a great pillar in each of its five corners and at the end was an enormous gate made of stone surrounded by carved decorations matching the style of the ones on the gate itself.

Matt ran towards it and tried to push it open. Hunter followed so that he could help out by pushing the heavy gate open but it was no use, the gate was locked.

"Look for a key," Hunter said to the others.

Him and Matt started searching for a key nearby.

"A key…? The door does not even have a keyhole," Kleo said wondering if the two of them were ever using the eyes they had in their skulls.

Both of them looked back at her, confused as they were, they went to the gate once more and pushed it even harder to see if it would open.

Kleo sighed.

She looked around trying to see if she could come up with a way to open the door. She decided to walk over and take a closer look at the carvings next to the gate. They pictured knights walking through the gate carrying the chest.

"Look… the gate looks different," she said while pointing to the one on the carving.

Matt and Hunter hurried over to take a closer look. In comparison to the real gate, this one had what appeared to be a wooden cross in the top center of the gate. They all looked up to see where the cross was supposed to be, and sure enough, it did seem as if something had once been placed up there.

"Maybe it fell down," Hunter said.

"Yeah, and then it vanished into thin air," Matt sassily replied. "If it fell down then where did it wander off too?" he asked him while rolling his eyes.

"Look around to see if it's here somewhere," Kleo said as she was trying to avoid them starting yet another discussion.

"Come on, buddy, let's go find it," she said encouragingly to the cub who was still staying as close to her as possible.

The hall was huge, and there were so many corners to search. They had not looked for long before the cub started howling.

"Can you make him be quiet?" Matt asked as he did not want to draw unnecessary attention towards them in case other wolves were nearby or maybe even a bear, if that was really the case.

Kleo tried to shush the cub, not knowing what was wrong. She sat down next to him, trying to give him a cuddle but he kept howling.

"Shh, you have to be quiet," she said and continued trying to calm him down, but the little cub did not give up the howling.

"Maybe he is hungry?" Hunter shouted from the other end of the hall.

Kleo got up and tried to see if there was any food in there that she could give him. As she approached a pile of boulder rocks in one of the corners, a mouse came running out from in between the gaps in the stones. The cub ran after it trying his very best to catch it. The mouse continued out of the hall and back the way they came, and before they knew it, both mouse and wolf, were gone.

"Great job," Matt said while being as surprised as she was with how fast that all just happened.

"He'll come back," she said with a bit of doubt as they all proceeded their search for the cross.

"This is hopeless," Hunter said and sat down. "There must be some other way to get it opened."

They all went back to the gate trying to see if there might be another clue hidden in there somewhere. None of it made sense to them, it was the same over and over, knights, the chest, the cross and that stupid oval stone again that they seemed to be so fond of. Matt noticed that the engraved symbols, that each pillar had in the middle, were all facing towards the gate in the carvings. He turned around and looked at the five pillars. Only three of them had their symbols facing the gate, the other two were facing away from it.

"Hunter, help me out for a second," he said as he walked towards the first pillar.

Hunter walked over to him. "What do you need me to do?"

"Help me turn this middle piece around," he said and grabbed onto it and started twisting the stone around.

It slowly gave in and as soon as it started moving around it was as if the whole room was moving with it. Hunter got a good grip and used all his strength to twist the piece. Now the symbol was facing the gate and in that very second the decorations on the bottom part of the gate moved and made a loud sound as if something inside was unlocking. Kleo ran to the next pillar helping them out by turning the middle piece around on that one too. Immediately after twisting the piece around the middle part of the gate did the exact same as the bottom half before. They all looked at each other smiling, they could not believe that they had figured it out. However, the gate still did not open. Once again Hunter and Matt went to see if they could force it open. Kleo looked around and saw that the cub was coming back to them, and quickly noticed that he was dragging something along in his mouth.

"What did you find," Kleo said while grabbing whatever was in his mouth. "I cannot believe it," she said.

The guys looked over to see what had gotten her so excited and quickly saw that she was standing with the cross in her hand.

"Where did he get that?" Hunter said while looking particularly surprised.

"I think what you might want to ask yourself is how we are going to get it all the way up there?" Matt said and looked up at the top of the gate.

From being the great climber that Kleo was, she had already laid out her route to get to the top of the gate. She fastened the cross in the side of her belt, laid the torch on the ground and started making her way to the top. The carvings on the gate definitely made it easier and almost effortless for her to get to the top as it was almost as if they were made for the job. They were all watching from the ground, Hunter and Matt were excited to finally get the door opened and the cub looked rather nervous as she was making her way to the top. She reached the top within seconds and got ready to place the cross in the dent where it once had been. It slid right into place, fitting perfectly, and as soon as it was in place the hinges on the door moved downwards and then sideways. Kleo quickly got down from the gate and got ready to push with the others.

They pushed and pushed using all their strength and the gate still would not move an inch.

"What is missing?" Matt shouted as he kicked the door in pure anger.

"Relax, we'll figure it out, we always figure it out," Kleo said without hesitation.

Hunter looked away and went over towards a stone to sit down for a little while. He had a sad look on his face, but it did not seem as if it had anything to do with the locked gate. Matt was pacing around the hall and Kleo was playing with the wolf who was running around jumping on the big boulder stones in the corner. You could feel the tension in the room as they were all twisting their minds trying to figure out what they had missed. Kleo went over to the stones where Hunter was sitting, and of course, the cub ran after her. As she started talking to him the little wolf jumped up trying to lick him in the face which he found rather annoying, so he got up on his feet.

"He likes you," she said.

As she looked down, she noticed that a big piece of Hunter's shirt had been ripped off.

"What happened there?" she asked him and pointed to where the shirt was missing a piece.

"Oh... uhm..." It was as if he did not know what to say. "I guess it must have ripped on a branch or something when we ran from the wolves," he then said with a nervous smile.

Matt was tired of pacing around and went to the gate taking one last look at the drawings.

"There must be a way," he mumbled to himself as he scraped his fingers across the carvings. He looked closely and noticed three loose rocks in the gate. He touched one of them and noticed that it seemed as if the stone could be pushed further inside. He gently pressed on it and sure enough it went deeper inside the gate. He was shocked yet quickly pushed the other two and immediately stepped back as the entire gate started moving towards him. Kleo and Hunter got interrupted with their conversation from the loud noise coming from the gate and they both hurried over to Matt.

It was finally opening.

"Great, another large room," Hunter said as he took a peek inside.

On each side of the room were what appeared to be tubs of tar. Matt rushed over and grabbed a torch from the wall that he used to light the tar on fire, without even wondering how the torches in the room were lit in the first place. It quickly ignited and the whole room started to light up as the tubs had tar-covered ropes hanging above them that was caught by the flame and led the flame to yet another tub further ahead. Besides the tubs there was nothing in the room.

It was completely empty.

All it had was a decorated stone floor and some statues in the walls on each side and at the far end there was yet another door. But the room itself was indeed empty.

"No treasure," Hunter said as he looked inside the empty room that created an echo from the sound of his voice.

Matt took a few steps inside the room and turned around looking at the others.

"Come on, let's keep moving," he said and took a few steps forward.

Kleo followed and Hunter came right after. The little cub ran out onto the floor a little ahead of the others. He did not get far before he hit some sort of plate in the floor. As the tiny wolf stepped on it with his paw the plate sank further down into the floor.

All three of them saw the plate sink, and the little wolf ran over and hit between Kleo's legs. Matt made a sign for them to stand still as a clicking sound of gears turning emerged from inside the walls.

"This does not seem good," Hunter said in the background.

Kleo looked around at the statues in the walls. Their mouths and eyes were opening, and something was moving inside of the dark dents.

"Down," she yelled as loud as she could while quickly dropping to the floor tucking the cub into her body attempting to keep him safe.

Matt and Hunter barely got to the ground before arrows were shooting out from the statues and through the room. Luckily none of them were hit.

The shooting arrows had stopped and slowly they all got back up on their feet.

"Great, so how do we get across without being killed by a bunch of murderous statues from hell?" Hunter asked with a slight irritation in his voice.

"We could crawl across?" Kleo suggested as it did not seem as if any of the arrows were shot below knee height.

"No, maybe none of the arrows were low this time, but further ahead the statues look different so we shouldn't risk it. We should just run across," Matt said while looking at both of the others.

"Run?" Hunter burst out while looking at him as if he expected Matt to be joking.

"Yes, we run it," Matt repeated. "Before when he stepped on the plate with his paw it took at least a few seconds before the arrows were shot, so if we all sprint towards the door at the same time then it will not matter if we hit the plates as the arrows will be shooting behind us anyway."

"What about him?" Kleo said while looking down at the wolf.

"Well, he is for sure faster than we are, so we will just have to trust that he will follow along."

"And if he doesn't"? Hunter asked him with a lot of doubt in his eyes about Matt's idea.

Kleo looked at Matt giving him a slight nod showing that she trusted his plan.

"Get ready to run, furball," Matt said as he looked down at the cub who sat so politely on the floor while all three of them got in their positions.

"This better work," Hunter said while taking a deep breath.

"Ready?" Matt asked looking towards the others for confirmation and, before they knew it, they were running. Each of them stepped on multiple of the sinking plates as they ran, and they could all feel the wind from the arrows shooting right behind them.

"AH!" it sounded from Hunter as they were running.

They reached the end of the room and pulled the door open and got in the next room as fast as they could.

"What happened?" Kleo asked as she turned around to check on Hunter.

She was met with a rather unpleasant sight. Hunter had an

arrow stuck in his left shoulder. He took a few deep breaths before he pulled it out. Luckily the wound was not too deep, however, it was still bleeding a lot and the white sleeve of his shirt turned red in an instant.

"Great plan," he said while throwing the arrow to the ground.

"Well, it got us through, didn't it?" Matt asked him as he was clearly annoyed with him and his complaining.

"Next time, you listen to her. If we had just crawled across the arrow would never have hit me," he said while clearly still being upset about what happened and the fact that Matt was the one in charge.

"Maybe you should just learn to run a little faster?" Matt said which was clearly an attempt to provoke him.

Hunter went towards Matt and pushed him in pure anger. Matt quickly threw a punch back at him and, before Kleo had a chance to do anything, they were fighting. The wolf started howling again as he was clearly unhappy with them being as aggressive as they were.

"Stop it!" Kleo yelled a few times which eventually made both the guys take down their guards and walk away from each other.

She went towards Hunter trying to see to his wound.

"Can you guys just please behave nicely towards one another and stop acting like kids for at least five minutes?" she said with a firm voice making them both feel stupid.

They had all been so busy fighting that none of them had looked around the room which they had just entered. Matt was speechless from what he saw. The entire room was glowing up from the torches made from solid gold that were hanging on the walls and from the chandeliers dangling down from the ceiling.

Hunter went over and tried to lift one of the torches but failed to do so as they were too heavy for a single man to carry. The room itself was magnificent with all its golden details. It even had a staircase in the end leading up to a door decorated with a golden dragon.

It was a truly and utterly beautiful sight.

The treasure had to be close by. All three of them could feel it. They slowly approached the stairs being on alert in case any unwanted surprises were going to come out from the walls again. Soon they had reached the door and it took all of them a few deep breaths before they were ready to see what was waiting for them on the other side. The door needed a bit of a push in order for it to open. It had obviously been a long time since anyone had entered, causing the hinges to have rusted together a bit.

They finally walked though and sure enough there it was. Right in the middle of the room on a platform stood the golden chest. It was glowing with color from the gems, shining like nothing any of them had ever seen. They all looked at each other, with relief and they were indeed proud to have actually found it.

Chapter Nine

Enzo had reached the entrance to the cave. He and his men were about to enter as soon as the horses had been secured outside, along with the carriage, that they were going to be using to carry the treasure back to the camp at the shore, that two of the horses had been towing along the way there. They took a close look at the carvings outside next to the entrance, but Enzo did not seem to care much for what they meant. He had only one thing on his mind, which was to find the treasure as fast as possible.

Some of the men were about to light a number of torches before they marched away into the darkness. Carrying both swords and shields, the men were prepared to enter the depths of the cave and face whatever might come their way. As they set foot inside Henry walked up to Enzo and put his hand on his shoulder as a sign of pride over what he was about to achieve.

"We're almost there," Henry said to him.

"Yes, I am," Enzo replied, which gave Henry an uncertain look on his face.

***

They were about to approach the treasure. While the three of them slowly walked towards the chest, they all kept a tight lookout through the room and paid full attention to the floor making sure no more surprises would come shooting out of the walls.

Hunter's arm had almost stopped bleeding and his mood had gotten better since the search was finally over. Matt and Kleo were both completely stunned, they never really expected to be able to find the treasure, let alone find it before being caught by Enzo and his men.

It was only now they began to realize that they had not given any thought to how they were supposed to get the treasure out of there, or even where to hide it to avoid it getting into Enzo's hands.

Matt and Hunter went up the steps to the platform where the treasure was standing in all its pride and tried to open it up so that they could get a glimpse of what truly laid inside. The chest was of course locked, which they should have expected it to be.

They tried everything but no matter what they did the chest remained locked.

In the meantime, Kleo and the wolf had been walking around the room checking for other items that may be hidden there. Maybe there would even be a key laying around somewhere. She did not find anything besides what seemed to be a stone of some sort that looked more like an egg really and it was placed on a lone table in the far end of the room being almost invisible compared to the chest.

Kleo felt like she had seen something like this before, but she did not seem to quite remember where. It was broken in the middle and, if it was in fact an egg, it had hatched a long time ago considering the amount of dust and spider webs on the outside, which was also in the way and made it impossible to see how truly beautiful it was. The inside of it was mesmerizing, it had small shiny crystals all around the inside glowing and sparkling from the light that lit up the room.

She called for Matt to get over and check out what she had

found as she finally remembered where she had seen it before.

Hunter stayed with the chest still trying to find a way to open it.

"What is it?" Matt asked as he walked towards her.

"Look at this," she said while handing over the stone to him. He looked at it with a curious face.

"A stone," he said with a frown on his face from confusion as to why she seemed so excited about a stone when it was even broken in the middle.

"Don't you recognize it?" she asked him with an excited expression on her face hoping that it would soon come to his mind.

He looked at her waiting for her to tell him as he had no clue as to where she was going with this.

"It is the oval stone from the carvings in the walls. I know it's broken now but it's for sure the same one," she said while waiting for him to finally keep up with her.

"You think it is valuable?" he whispered when he realized that it actually could be the same stone, and he did not want Hunter to see it.

"I don't know but I don't think that whoever made the decorations on the walls would have carved it if it wasn't at least important," she said.

"Look! over here," Hunter shouted from the other side of the room. He had found a hidden stairway leading down further into the ground. Kleo brought the stone as they walked to see where the stairs led.

The old wooden stairway went far down into the deep. All they could see was a tiny bit of light and the end of it.

"Maybe the key is down there," Hunter said while looking at the others, not noticing the somewhat large stone in her hands.

"We cannot leave the treasure out of sight," Matt said while looking back over his shoulder at the chest.

"I will stay and look after it," Hunter said.

Matt did not seem happy with the idea of leaving him alone with the treasure as he still did not fully trust him.

"I'm not leaving you alone with it," Matt said to him.

"Oh, I see. You still don't trust me," he said irritated.

"No, I don't," Matt said, not giving a great deal about hurting his feelings.

"Matt!" Kleo said being disappointed with how he, once again, was treating Hunter.

"No, I get it. I only saved Kleo from drowning when you were not able to and found the entrance to the cave for that matter," Hunter said while turning around to walk away.

Kleo stared at Matt trying to make him realize how unfairly he was being towards Hunter.

"If I wanted the treasure for myself, why would I have called for you as soon as I found the entrance?" he said as he turned back around trying to confront Matt.

Matt stared into the ground being ashamed after he could clearly see Hunter's point in what he had just said. If he truly wanted the treasure for himself, he had for sure had the chance to do so.

"Fine. You stay here while we go down and check it out," Matt said to him in a very modest way.

"Okay, let's get going then," Kleo said as she looked at Hunter acknowledging that he should stay behind.

Matt went first, followed by the little wolf and Kleo who was carrying the stone under her arm. It seemed as if there was no end to the wiggling staircase leading further and further down. They both thought that they heard footsteps further ahead, however, nobody was to be seen on the stairs. They reached the end after some time and the stairs had led them to a great tunnel. Torches were flickering with fire, and since they were not the ones who had lit them, there had to be someone else walking around down there. As they slowly walked through the tight tunnel, they could see spiders crawling all over the walls and ceiling that were covered with webs, and they could hear the flickering wings of the moths that were flying around their heads.

At the end of the tunnel, they found yet another door. Underneath the gap in the door, they could see light moving around. The little wolf started growling at a moving shadow behind the door. They both put forth their weapons getting ready to enter, not knowing what was on the other side. Matt reached for the handle and took a deep breath before opening the door. Slowly they peeked inside to see if there was anybody walking around in there, but it seemed to be empty.

They both took a step forth into what appeared to be an old library of sorts with shelves all around the room with old books and scrolls full of dust. Since the coast was clear they decided to look around. Kleo went to the middle of the room to take a look at an open book that was laying on an old wooden desk while Matt went through all the shelves in search of a key.

The book had a drawing of an oval stone, the same as the one she had found, and according to the book the stone was called a septarian. It showed the stone as a whole and underneath it had yet another drawing of a stone, broken, in the exact same way as the one she had in her possession.

"Uhm, Matt," she said with a nervous voice looking at him as he walked over to her. He looked down at the book where the drawing of the septarian was and read the page about it. Matt had a tense look on his face as he slowly turned to the next page.

On the page it had a drawing at the bottom of the stone, the septarian, that had cracked open like an egg.

"You believe it's an egg," Matt said as he looked at her with a worried expression on his face.

"I'm not sure. But what worries me is the fact that if this truly is an egg, it has obviously already hatched, but what creature came out of it, and where is it now?" she said while pointing her finger at the drawing of the cracked stone.

The wolf started growling again. Matt and Kleo turned around in fear of what was behind them. Kleo had grasped her sword and Matt was ready to aim with his bow. As soon as they turned around, they were taken by surprise.

A knight was standing not too far away from them. He had a beard and hair which both looked neatly groomed, he was wearing armor covered with a white robe decorated with a red cross. In one side of his belt, he had a sword and in the other a dagger.

Where he had come from neither of them knew as they had been facing the entrance the entire time and no one had entered for sure.

"I see you found the septarian," the knight said with a deep yet calm voice.

They both had an odd look and their faces and looked over at the stone with wonder, yet neither of them provided him with an answer as they were too busy trying to assess whether they should trust him or if he was up to something since, they had no clue of who he was.

"My name is Elyas. I am one of the many protectors of the last septarian. You need not fear me," he said while slowly walking towards them.

Kleo put away her sword and had Matt lower his bow.

"Are you also the protector of the chest?" Kleo asked him curiously.

"I was the protector of the chest," he said while looking at the egg Kleo had placed on the desk.

"Was?" Matt asked him, puzzled as he was.

"The chest is empty and is nothing but a decoy," Elyas said. "Well, not entirely empty, but nothing of value lays inside... Follow me," he said and simply turned around with the expectation that they would follow him.

Kleo and Matt looked at each other with surprise. Could it really be true that they had risked their lives for a chest that proved to be empty this entire time? And why would a man tell them all of this without even knowing who they were?

Elyas walked towards one of the bookshelves that had a statue next to it. As he grabbed the statue by the hand the entire bookshelf began to move. It must have been that hidden door from whence he came. Kleo and Matt both looked at each other before following the knight through the hidden door which they were doubting to be a good idea at the time. They both had a skeptical look on their faces but neither of them could hide the fact that they were curious to figure out what exactly was going on. The door led to another tunnel, this one was thankfully less spooky as it was without spiders and webs all around. The little wolf followed the knight into the tunnel and stayed close to him as he seemed to already like him, which was also the reason that made Kleo trust him. At least enough to follow him without thinking too much about the consequence.

While they were walking through the tunnel Elyas did not speak a single word. Kleo walked next to the cub and Matt walked in the far back and kept his hand close to his sword the whole time. He had tried to ask a few questions to the knight about the empty treasure chest but had not yet had any luck getting a response from him.

***

In the chamber above, Hunter was still trying his best to break the chest open. How the chest could even be locked without it even having an actual keyhole he could not understand. There had to be some way to open it.

He went over to the stairway where the others had gone down. They had been gone for quite some time and he could not see or hear them at the end. He was trying to decide whether he should go down to check on them or stay behind to keep an eye on the chest like he had promised. He paced back and forth a few times while chewing one of his fingernails in frustration. He could not make himself leave the chest unguarded and break the promise he had made, especially not now after he finally had gained Matt's trust. At least a little bit.

As he walked back towards the chest, he got the idea that maybe he could carry the chest and hide it somewhere safe. He tried both to push the chest and lift it, however, it was too heavy for him to do alone. The sweat was almost dripping from his forehead since he used all his strength to get it to move but nothing happened, it had not even moved an inch.

He sat down on the ground next to the chest debating with himself about what to do. What if something had happened to them and they needed his help?

Just as he was about to run down the stairway, he heard faint voices coming from far away. The voices were not from the end of the stairs, it came from the path they had followed to get here. He got a tense look on his face as he went closer attempting to listen to who made the sounds. It sounded like moving armor and loud footsteps in the distance. Fortunately, judging from the faint noise, there was still time for Kleo and Matt to return. Hunter looked back at the chest a few times while standing in the doorway listening to the voices.

"What have I done?" Hunter mumbled to himself with a nervous look on his face as he looked towards the staircase in hopes that Kleo and Matt would appear.

Chapter Ten

Elyas had led Kleo and Matt to the end of the tunnel where they were now facing an old wooden door. Before they entered, he had politely requested that they would stay completely calm when they entered the next room. The cub could smell something and seemed rather intrigued by whatever was awaiting them on the other side.

Matt and Kleo were still a bit confused by the whole situation and Matt still could not get past the fact that they had been looking for an empty treasure all this time.

As Elyas slowly opened the door Kleo and Matt tried to peek inside to see what was in there, however, all they could see was a great stone hall, almost the size of a castle, and it had canyons reaching even further underground. While entering the great hall, Elyas finally started talking.

"Centuries ago, a stone of great importance was found in the desert and brought here, far away from civilization, for safekeeping. Only our ancestors knew about the location of the stone and where it was being kept until not so long ago when one of our fellow knights chose to sell the information in return for a small amount of gold. No map ever existed of this island until that day, and we have tried to get our hands on it ever since. I can only assume that, from you two being here, the map has been somewhere along your path."

"Yes," Matt said, acknowledging to Elyas that he had seen it.

"What was it that they had found in the desert?" Kleo asked him curiously as she was fascinated by his story and wanted to hear more.

"They found the septarian that you left on the desk in the library. We believe it was the last living sample of its kind," he said to her as they walked towards the center of the hall.

"Living? I thought you said it was a stone?" Matt asked while sounding slightly frightened.

"What exactly is a septarian?" Kleo wondered out loud.

"You ask a question to which you already know the answer," Elyas said astounded.

"An egg," she said as she had understood that part so far, however, she was more interested in knowing what sort of egg it was.

"You said you used to be the protector of the chest but now you protect what it once held, so how come the stone, egg I mean, was laying on the ground upstairs being all dusty like it had no value," Matt asked him with suspicion.

Before he got an answer, they heard a huge roar coming from the bottom of the canyon followed by the sound of wind coming from a large wingspan. The little wolf got scared and ran behind Kleo's legs.

"Because the value is no longer inside of it," Elyas said with a smile looking out towards the sound, and whistled.

Kleo and Matt both looked at each other, frightened, when nothing less than a huge dragon came flying towards them. They were both frozen and were unable to move from being completely petrified.

The dragon was enormous. The scales were silver and almost shined as if they were a newly polished armor, it almost looked as if the dragon was made of steel. It had spikes throughout the tail and great claws on its feet. The wings looked the same as those of a bat, however, these were obviously bigger. On its head, it had what looked like a magnificent crown, formed by multiple pointy horns and the eyes were bright and huge, and their color was even more blue than Kleo's.

"Do not fear him, he means you no harm," Elyas said, attempting to calm both of them down.

The dragon flew right above their heads and landed on the ground behind them. They all turned around quickly and were unable to take their eyes of it. Neither of them said a word, they just stood there for a minute while the wind from the dragon's breath was flowing smoothly through their hair. The little wolf had decided to be the courageous one in the pack and started approaching the dragon a bit.

"How do you know he won't harm us?" Matt said to Elyas.

"He has been with us since he hatched. He has been trained well and he has no reason to harm us for we have not done anything to harm him," Elyas said.

"Trained him? Whoever has the guts for that must be rather staunch," Matt said.

Kleo went a few steps closer to the dragon as she was after all quite mesmerized by him, which seemed to make Matt rather nervous. The dragon put his head closer to her and looked deep into her eyes.

"He knows he can trust you, Kleo," Elyas said to her.

"Trust me? Wait, how do you know my name?" she asked him baffled.

"I knew your father," Elyas said which caused Matt to put his hand around his sword once again as he never failed to show that he did not trust anyone.

Kleo had a troubled and confused look on her face, how did

a knight who lived in a cave know her father, a fisherman, from a small village? However, she remained silent hoping that Elyas would elaborate.

"Your father was one of the knights who helped protect the dragon. The day his ship sank it got caught in the storm that roams around the coasts of this island. He was on his way back home to you and your mother," he said to her.

Kleo stood for a few seconds not knowing what to say.

"Her father was a fisherman," Matt said, yet with his hand ready to draw his sword.

"Her father was a dragon lord," Elyas said. "You look a lot like your father, not only your eyes, but I can tell that you are as fierce as he was," Elyas said.

It took Kleo a while to take in the information. She just stood for a while looking at the dragon not really knowing what to believe. She knew there had to be some truth to his words, because how could he possibly know that Kleo got her blue eyes from her father and not her mother and that her father had drowned at sea?

"Can't he fly out of this cave?" Matt asked.

"He is not trapped here; he can go if he means to. We have our own ways in and out of this cave," Elyas said.

Matt was truly fascinated by the dragon, which seemed to surprise him as he had always talked about how he never wanted to meet one in person. He had heard many stories about them but never expected any bit of it to be true and he truly believed that they did not exist.

"Can he spit fire?" Matt asked excited.

"Yes," Elyas said.

"Does he have a name?" Matt then asked. He clearly had many questions about the creature.

"We call him Alvaro," Elyas said.

"Alvaro," Kleo said while looking the dragon in his eyes. The dragon took a step forward, which appeared to frighten Matt a bit since he took a step backwards, but Kleo did not move an inch as the dragon approached her.

"You can pet him if you would like to," Elyas said, "He enjoys it very much."

Kleo looked at Elyas as if she still doubted his words, but she had never before had an encounter with a dragon, let alone got a chance to touch one, so she obviously could not help herself. She slowly put forth her hand and gently placed it on the side of the dragon's face and gave him a pet. As she touched the dragon her eyes sparkled with pure happiness, it felt so natural to her, and she did not for one second feel insecure or frightened.

Elyas smiled from the sight of her and the dragon, he believed her to have the same gifts as her father and this only acknowledged his theory even further. Matt on the other hand was quite unsure about the situation, in spite of him finding the dragon rather cool, it did not for a second mean that he trusted it. Kleo took a few steps back after petting him and looked at her hand. The feeling she had in her palm was like nothing she had ever felt before, it almost felt magical. It was like a tingling but also filled with heat. Elyas noticed her looking at her hand and slowly blinked to the dragon as a sign of confirmation. After both of them had taken it all in for a few moments, Kleo turned around and looked at Matt.

"Matt, we have to get back to Hunter, he's been guarding an empty chest this entire time and we need to tell him all this," Kleo said and started running towards the tunnel from where they came.

The wolf of course ran right after her while Matt on the other hand tried to stop her, but it did not help, he could do nothing but follow her back.

Elyas stayed behind with the dragon not seeming too worried with the whole event and them running off.

"She will come around," Elyas said to the dragon while he gently placed his hand on the dragon's side to give him a pet.

It did not take long before they were back in the library. Kleo was so busy running to the staircase that she even forgot to bring the septarian from the desk. Matt was not far behind, and the steps on the staircase were moving underneath their feet as they were running up as fast as they possibly could.

"Hunter!" Kleo shouted as they were almost at the top.

"Did you find a key?" Hunter asked them but he did not exactly look happy about the fact that they had returned.

"No," Matt said which seemed to give Hunter a bit of relief.

"You need to hear this," Kleo said but got interrupted from the loud sound of footsteps approaching them from the entrance.

"I'm so sorry," Hunter said and looked at her with regret in his eyes just before he took a few steps away from both of them.

Through the door came Enzo, marching along with his men. He immediately spotted the shiny chest when they walked inside the room.

"Well thank you my two lovebirds for leading me to my treasure," he said mockingly to Matt and Kleo. "You both did a very impressive job."

Matt and Kleo looked at each other both angry and disappointed, and slightly confused with how he had found the location of the treasure so fast.

"You didn't think that I would let you escape without keeping a close eye on you, did you now?" he said to provoke the two of them even further.

Matt and Kleo both noticed an eagle sitting on one of the men's shoulders. Henry's shoulder. It was the eagle they had seen a couple of times flying above them on their journey across the island and in his hand he held a piece of cloth matching Hunter's shirt.

"If you would be so kind as to all step aside," Enzo said while making a motion with his hand to have them back away from the chest.

Both Kleo and Matt stood their ground and did not move an inch. They both looked ready to put up a fight while Hunter did not move a muscle and just stood there in the background keeping his head facing the ground.

"Now," Enzo said demandingly and started walking towards them.

Matt realized that it made no sense to put up a fight with the number of men Enzo had brought along, so he grabbed Kleo by her wrist and gently led her away from the chest. Enzo smiled as he went towards the treasure and got ready to open it not knowing it was locked. Both Matt and Kleo got a small smile on their faces as they were quite enjoying seeing him struggle to open a chest not knowing that nothing was supposedly inside. Enzo was struggling to force the chest open and became more and more irritated. Matt accidentally let out a chuckle which immediately triggered Enzo who rushed towards them in an instant.

"Give me the key," he said to them while sticking his hand out ready for Matt to hand over the key as he assumed that is why he was laughing.

Matt did nothing and just stood still and gave Enzo a rather threatening look.

"Hand it over!" He yelled right in his face almost causing Matt to fall over backwards.

"We don't have a key," Kleo said and laid her hand on Enzo's chest as if she wanted to push him away from them.

Enzo looked down at her hand that was touching him and took a deep breath. Kleo realized that her touch was only provoking him even more, so she quickly retrieved her hand and swallowed nervously while cautiously staring at Enzo. He backed away from them without saying another word and went back to the chest. They could hear him mumbling to himself but no one in the room could tell what he was saying.

"Sir, let's just take the chest and go, we will find a way to force it open," Henry said in the back.

"I'm in charge here, I'm the one giving out orders," Enzo shouted back at him.

Henry bowed his head down with respect and took a step backwards. Nobody in the room dared to make another sound as everyone was afraid of what Enzo might do. Even his own men seemed frightened by him.

"Son, get over here, it's time to leave," Enzo said and looked at Hunter.

"Son?" Matt and Kleo said in chorus while looking at each other confused. They did not believe the words they had just heard. How could he be Enzo's son? Enzo did not even look old enough to have a son that age.

Hunter looked over at Kleo as he walked past her. He looked heartbroken with what he had done, and Kleo did not once look at him as he passed by her. She could not even bear to look at him as she had truly trusted him and stood up for him the entire time.

"You bastard, I knew you couldn't be trusted," Matt shouted and almost jumped Hunter. He would have succeeded if it had not been for Kleo who was fast enough to stop him. The situation would have escalated and become far worse for the two of them, more than it already was, and she did not want to risk that even though she felt like Hunter definitely deserved it in that very moment.

The fury in Matt's eyes was intense, even for Kleo, she had never seen him like this and was dreading what he might do next, so she did her best to keep him calm. Matt slowly stroked his arrows with his hand, and he would have been ready to take a shot if they had not been outnumbered. Hunter was walking towards his father without even looking at him and continued walking towards Henry where he stopped and stood next to him. The eagle jumped from Henry's shoulder over to Hunter's.

Neither Kleo nor Matt could believe what had just happened or how Hunter had managed to fool them to the extent that he had.

Enzo looked around the chest for a keyhole, but did not managed to find one. Frustrated as he was, he got up and ordered two of his men to get over and carry the treasure out.

The little wolf started growling and walked towards Enzo being unsatisfied with the presence of him and his men.

"I see you made a friend," Enzo said while pointing his sword at the cub.

Kleo drew her sword and rushed towards him threatening to kill him if he did anything to harm the wolf. Enzo gave a sign for his men to stand down and did not seem to care much about her threats, he seemed to rather enjoy her feisty and fierce behavior. He just stood there not taking his eyes off her while his men struggled to lift up the chest.

The two guards could not lift the chest on their own so Henry made two more walk over to help them out. After only a few attempts the chest finally got lifted from the ground. The entire room was shaking, and stones began to drop from the ceiling. The men hurried in order to carry the chest towards the door from where they came. The chest had been standing on a pressure plate and as soon as it was lifted off the ground the entire room started to collapse around them. The cub ran towards the stairway and giant stones fell in between Matt and the exit.

Kleo was still standing right in front of Enzo and just before a huge rock fell down just where she stood Enzo dragged her aside.

It did not take long before a big wall of stones had formed and separated the room in two halves. Matt and the wolf on one side, Kleo along with Enzo and his men on the other. Matt could not see anything from all the dust he had gotten into his eyes. Kleo pushed herself away from Enzo and ran towards the tall pile of stones. As the dust settled Matt ran to the stones and tried to climb over but the stones were moving too much causing him to fall down. He called out for Kleo to see if she was okay on the other side while desperately trying to find a way to get to her.

"I'm fine," she said back while also trying to find a way to climb over the stones.

"Well well, it looks like I get to bring more than one treasure home," Enzo said while reaching his hand out for Kleo to go with him.

She felt sick with his comment and tried to ignore him and instead of listening more to his inappropriate and provocative words, she instead tried to climb to the other side. As she attempted to climb the stones started moving causing her to fall down. She refused to give up and kept climbing back up but it was indeed impossible to get across.

Matt shouted from the other side for Enzo to leave Kleo alone while pushing and fighting with all the strength that he had in his body, struggling to get the stone wall to fall.

Enzo sighed and he was clearly out of patience. He gave a sign to his men to grab Kleo and get moving. As soon as the first guard grabbed her, she immediately started fighting them.

Enzo eventually cleared his throat in order to get Kleo's attention. She turned around and was met with the sight of three of his men aiming with ignited arrows to the side where Matt was standing.

In the same second as Kleo let down her guard she was grabbed by his men.

"Pretty eyes, you are coming with me whether you like it or not," Enzo said while walking towards the door along with the rest of his men. Hunter was standing in the doorway looking over at the side where Matt was, it seemed as if Hunter wanted to help him out but, when Enzo passed by him, he grabbed his son's arm firmly and forced him to walk along.

Matt could be heard yelling from the other side but there was nothing he could do to help.

Kleo and the others had already reached the room with the arrow-shooting statues. She got rather nervous from seeing three of Enzo's men dead on the floor pierced with arrows.

"Shields up!" Henry ordered as they were about to walk through.

The men all got into formation with their shields, making sure the entire group was covered from all angles before they walked through the room. While walking, the sound of hundreds of arrows could be heard hitting the shields from all direction and after safely getting through, they all continued to make their way safely out of the cave.

Chapter Eleven

Matt sat on the ground exhausted after trying to break down the wall. Next to him sat the little wolf looking at him as if he could not understand why Kleo was not coming back. Matt was trying to figure out a way to get out of there, and just as he was about to give it one more attempt to break down the stone wall, he remembered what Elyas had told them. He had said that the knights used other entrances so there had to be another way out of there.

He got up so fast that he saw both moon, sun, and stars around him for a second before he was able to get moving. He told the cub to come along as he ran towards the stairs to get back down and find Elyas. They reached the library in no time and continued over towards the hidden door behind the shelves. Matt grabbed the hand of the statue, just like he had seen Elyas do, to make the door open up, but it did not work. He tried a few more times, placing his hands in different ways to see what might work, but it still did not open.

He knocked on the door while shouting for Elyas to open up and let him through. He waited for quite some time without anything happening. He knocked harder and harder on the door hoping for Elyas to hear him. After a while with still nothing happening, he sat down on the floor next to the cub and gave him a few pets on the head.

"We'll find a way to get out of here, don't worry," he said trying to comfort both himself and the wolf who was staring at him with its big puppy eyes.

"Since you're sticking along you should have a name don't you think?" Matt said with a smile as the cub laid down resting his head on Matt's lab.

Matt sat for a while petting the tired wolf trying to come up with a good name for him.

"Your name could be Osbert," Matt said all of a sudden while looking down at the wolf checking to see if he actually did look like an Osbert.

The wolf lifted its head up and licked Matt's hand.

"Okay, Osbert it is," he said with a smile.

Just as Matt was beginning to consider the fact that they were trapped down there, the shelf started moving and the door was finally opening. Matt quickly got himself and Osbert back on their feet getting ready to enter the tunnel. To their surprise Elyas was not there, in fact no one was there, so he must have opened it from somewhere else. They ran as fast as they could to the other end where they were met by Elyas along with two other knights.

Both of the knights were dressed the exact same way as Elyas. Everything was identical. Matt was breathing heavily trying his best to explain to them what had happened upstairs panting the words out of his mouth.

"Come along," Elyas said, without fully understanding the nonsense that came out of Matts mouth, and they all started moving through the hall while the confused young man still tried his best to explain it all.

All three of the knights casually walked through the hall acting as if they could not see a giant dragon staring right at them. Matt stayed cautious while walking past the dragon as he did not exactly feel safe turning his back on it.

"Osbert, get over here," Matt whispered as the little wolf was about to make his way straight towards the dragon.

Even though Osbert strongly wanted to walk over and give the dragon a sniff, he still returned to Matt the very instant he called for him. The dragon, however, seemed to be rather curious with the unusually fluffy four-legged creature that was approaching him. Osbert caught up with Matt as they had reached a strong metal door in the far end of the hall. One of the knights slowly opened up the heavy door and they all entered a large chamber in which there were enormous amounts of silver, gold, weapons, and armor, enough to fit a small army.

Matt could not believe his eyes. He cared not for the gold and other valuables in there, he was far more amazed with all the weapons, and chainmail, and especially the longbows and helmets. Curiously he walked around gazing upon all the items in the room, he was so focused that he had not even noticed that Elyas and the other knights had continued into the next room. He looked over his shoulder as he picked up a sword and looked back, only to realize that the others were gone. As he put the sword back too quickly it resulted in five more falling to the ground making quite some noise. Matt wrinkled his face and closed his eyes firmly as they all dropped on the ground. Before picking them up he looked over his shoulder once again to check if Elyas had walked up behind him. Fortunately, it was only him and Osbert.

"Shh, don't tell them," Matt said to the wolf while giving a modest wink before he quickly ran to the next room trying to catch up with the others and acted as if nothing had happened.

Matt reached the next room where Elyas stood in front of a table with a map and was surrounded by at least ten other knights. Matt wondered where all these knights kept appearing from and how many of them were here on this, apparently not so lonely, island.

"Come," Elyas said while giving Matt a sign to approach the table.

Osbert stayed in the doorway while Matt slowly walked closer to the others. As he got closer to the table, he started to be able to see what was on the map. It looked like tunnels. Not just a few though. The map was full of tunnels, and it seemed as if the tunnels were also on different levels under the ground. All the knights greeted Matt as he approached them. He had a rather uncomfortable look on his face as if he was not quite sure whether or not something bad was about to happen.

"We will prepare the horses and take the tunnel right here," Elyas said while pointing to one of the many tunnels on the map. "You said this guy Enzo laid ship somewhere around here, correct?" he asked while looking up at Matt and pointed around the beach area where Enzo had in fact not only made port, but also built his camp.

Matt just nodded as he was too distracted to let any words out of his mouth. He was too busy looking around at all the knights and he could barely believe that he was standing in a cave underground, on an island, in a room full of knights. All the knights were extremely muscular and tall, not that they were giants, but they were definitely hugely built and extremely tall compared to Matt. He was indeed a muscular and very strong young man himself, but he could not exactly brag about his height. He used to be taller than Kleo when they were kids, but as they grew up, she had grown a bit taller than him if he had to be completely honest. Elyas and the knights were planning an attack on Enzo's camp, to not only retrieve Kleo, but also to get back the golden chest. As the chest was nothing but a decoy and a fake, of sorts, it did not have any great value besides the jewels on the outside, however, if Enzo was to sell the chest to someone who had little knowledge about it, he would still be able to get a decent amount of money for it.

It did not take long before they had planned everything thoroughly and were about to go back to the other chamber and prepare their weapons and armor. Elyas called for Matt to follow him. They walked towards the armor, and he reached for a chainmail that looked as if it could suit him just fine.

"Try it on," Elyas said while passing the chainmail to Matt.

Matt's eyes shone from being so excited and he could not believe that he was about to put on a real knight's armor. He was not lucky enough to get one of their white robes, but he did get a shield to fit with his sword and he was also given some of their arrows for his bow. He tried on one of their helmets as well but since he had never worn one before he was quite surprised with how small the holes for the eyes were, it felt as if his entire vision got blocked, he could not even see to the sides, so he quickly decided that it would be best to leave the helmet behind.

"Here," Elyas said while Matt was adjusting his armor.

He presented Matt with a beautiful sword. Matt took it in his hand to see how it felt.

"Thank you. But I think I prefer my own," he said and passed the sword back to Elyas.

As Elyas took back the sword he bowed, accepting Matt's choice, before laying the sword aside. Another knight approached them and gave Matt and Osbert some food and water so that they could regain their strength. He had even provided Osbert with a small blanket so that he could stay warm while sleeping in the corner of the room while the knights prepared themselves. Matt walked over to the cub trying to explain that he had to stay behind and that small wolves did not belong in battle.

He was surprised with himself for the fact that he felt sad about leaving the wolf behind, he had not expected that he would have grown to care for him. Osbert looked at Matt with sad eyes as if he understood that Matt was planning to leave him.

The knights were all ready to go and Elyas called for Matt to follow. He gave Osbert a few last pets, before he got up and started walking towards the exit. Matt looked back a few times checking that the wolf in fact did stay behind and he almost went through the door before he looked back one last time. Osbert was sitting in the corner with his head tilted to the side and his happy cub face had turned all sad.

"Who am I kidding?" Matt mumbled to himself while looking into the ground.

He looked back at the wolf in the corner and shook his head as if he was disagreeing with himself.

"Come on, Osbert, let's go and get Kleo back," he said while clapping his thigh a few times making Osbert run towards him as fast as he could. The wolf had the happiest look on his face while they were catching up with Elyas and the others further down the hallway.

***

Enzo and his men were long gone and had reached the end of the cave hours ago where their horses had been waiting for them. They had been riding at a great pace dragging along the still unopened chest that was being transported on the carriage attached to two horses. After already reaching the other side of the mountain they only needed to get through the forest before they were back at the camp on the beach. Kleo was all the way in the back sitting behind Shirtless on a horse riding next to

Whitefoot. She was still trying to take in all that Elyas had told them back in the cave and she was worried sick about Matt and Osbert. All she could do was to hope that they were unharmed and had found their way back to Elyas who could hopefully help them find a way out of there. Voices could be heard talking further ahead, which had caught Kleo's attention, and she slowly tilted to the side trying to see what was going on. It was not really clear to her, she only saw Hunter riding up towards the front, catching up with his father and Henry.

There was no way Kleo was going to go with Enzo, let alone Hunter, so she was trying to think of a way to escape before they reached the camp. Enzo kept turning his head around looking at her, almost as if he knew she was going to make a move. She needed to do something and it had to be now. Her hands were tied with rope, and she needed to figure out a way to get her hands free.

Kleo started twisting her hands around and desperately tried to wiggle the rope loose.

"Hey! stop doing that," Whitefoot said as he saw her trying to get the rope off.

"It's too tight, it hurts," she said, hoping that he would be dumb enough to loosen the knots for her.

Shirtless stopped his horse while Whitefoot tried to see if he could do something about the rope.

"What is going on down there?" Henry shouted, causing everybody to stop their horses from walking further.

Hunter rode down to them to see what the fuss was about with Enzo still keeping a close eye on him from up front.

"Just take it off," Hunter said to the twins.

"But..." Shirtless said before he was quickly cut off by Hunter.

"Take it off, she can't run off anyway," Hunter said while trying to make eye contact with her.

Though she was not very fond of his presence she still looked at him while getting her hands free as she wanted to look him in the eyes and show him exactly how she felt about him. It almost looked as if Hunter actually wanted her to escape judging by the look that he was giving her.

"Get moving," Enzo shouted and kicked his horse on the side to get going.

As all the men continued riding, Hunter leaned in trying to tell Kleo something.

"Hunter, get up here," his father yelled from afar.

He ignored his father at first and was about to open his mouth.

"Now!" Enzo yelled impatiently as he did not quite trust his son's intentions.

Hunter looked angry with his father but yet quickly turned his horse around and rode to the front. Kleo could tell from the look in Hunter's eyes that he wanted her to make a move and now that her hands were free it was certainly easier for her to do so.

Slowly she reached for the dagger in her boot, hoping no one around her would notice, which was especially hard with Whitefoot around, who was still riding next to her and was keeping a close eye on her every move. It was difficult to get the dagger out without making any big movements as it was somehow stuck inside her boot. Just as she got the dagger loose, Whitefoot turned his head as he had noticed she was up to something. She acted as if she was just trying to itch her ankle while hiding the dagger inside her hand. He did not seem to think much of it, and he soon turned his head back around, so he had thankfully not seen the dagger. As soon as she got the chance, she moved further back on the horse's back so that she was sure she was no longer on the saddle. She took a deep breath while closing her eyes getting ready to make her great escape and was praying for it to go well.

Quickly she slit the saddle strap making both Shirtless and the saddle fall to the ground. Enzo quickly stopped and turned around to see what was causing all the commotion in the back, but all he saw was Kleo grabbing the reins and riding away on one of the horses in high speed with Shirtless rolling around on the ground. Whitefoot was in shock and quickly jumped off his horse to help his brother back on his feet.

"You three, after her," Enzo ordered his men while looking into the forest watching Kleo disappear in between the trees. He had a glint in his eyes and a crooked smile on his face. It was as if he almost enjoyed her being noncompliant.

She rode as fast as she could, almost flying through the woods trying to get as far away from Enzo as possible, even though she had no idea in what direction to go. While continuously looking back over her shoulder to see if Enzo or any of his men were on her tail it did not take long before she noticed the three guards chasing her.

She was struggling to lead the horse through the trees and away from the path, and the three guards were quickly gaining up on her. They were spreading out trying to cut her off in every direction making it harder for her to maneuver her way around them.

Her horse was panting, almost being out of breath, and the men were getting too close, so she quickly made the horse break, turn around and run back the way they came, attempting to confuse the guards making them waste time with turning their horses back around too. It did not go as planned, they had soon caught up with her again and as she looked back over her shoulder the horse stopped as it had gotten one of its legs tangled in a thornbush. Before she had time to react, the horse stood up on its hind legs causing Kleo to fall to the ground before it ran off on its own. She quickly got herself untangles and was left with no other option but to run, they would catch up with her in no time but that did not scare her away from at least giving it a shot.

Without further thought she began to sprint through the forest as fast as her legs could possibly carry her. She managed to get quite far before the three guards had caught up with her on their horses. They used the horses to cut her off and were once again blocking her in each direction. As they jumped down from their horses' backs, they drew their swords and slowly approached her. She too went for her sword and looked around in all directions to keep an eye on each of the guards and, just as she was about to get attacked, they all got interrupted

"Leave her alone," a voice shouted behind them.

The men put down their swords in the very second that the order had been given to them and they all backed away from her with disappointed looks on their faces since they wanted to give her exactly what they thought that she deserved. As Kleo turned around to see who had yelled, she did not seem to be too surprised with who she saw. It was Hunter. He had followed them to make sure no harm was to come to her.

He reached his hand out to help her get on the back of his horse, but she rejected his offer and started wandering off instead. Hunter smiled as he could not help but to find her hard-to-get act slightly amusing. She did not manage to go far before Enzo and the rest of his men had arrived. She knew she once again did not have any other option but to go with them which, for good reason, both scared her and made her angry to say the least.

***

Matt was surprised to see the number of knights, there were at least fifty men walking in front of him, all in armor and ready to fight. They walked down a steep hill leading them down into the next tunnel. This tunnel was huge. It would definitely be possible to fit an entire dragon through there, he thought.

"This tunnel leads all the way from the dragon's den and out to the forest by the beach," Elyas said while pointing in the direction that led back to the dragon.

Matt did not seem fond of the thought that a dragon could potentially catch up with them in the tunnel and he would have nowhere to escape. He just had to stay focused and continue walking. However, he did feel as if the walk was going to take an entire day, at least, since it did after all reach almost all the way back to the beach where he had been days ago. After walking only for a short while, someone up front ordered them to stop. Matt, being all the way in the back, could not see much for the tall knights in front of him, so he had absolutely no idea of what was going on up there causing them to stand still.

They had passed a door on their right that one of the knights had opened and out walked a group of horses. Each knight took his horse, got up and prepared themselves to ride out the rest of the way. Matt was confused with how the knights were keeping horses hidden inside some mysterious closet far under the surface. How were the horses even staying alive in there?

As Matt approached Elyas, who was waiting for him at the door with a horse for each of them, Matt quickly peeked inside as he could not help but wonder if the horses were actually living in there. He could not believe his eyes. He even blinked a few times just in case his mind was playing tricks on him. It was definitely not a closet, not even close. Now Matt was not one to believe in magic or mythical creatures, or anything else for that matter, even though he had just met a dragon. But this for sure made him wonder if there was more to the world than he had grown up to believe. On the other side of the door was, to Matt's big surprise, a huge underground forest.

It was the most astonishing thing he had ever seen. Tall trees arose from the ground, grass was growing on the stones making it look as if they were small hills, flowers were blooming next to a bright blue lake and even a waterfall was falling from the sky. Sunlight peeked down through a hole in the ground above them and shined upon the horses and birds that were living there. The air from within was the freshest and cleanest breath of air Matt had ever taken in, he could not help but take a few extra deep breaths before Elyas closed the door. They both got up on their horses and Matt took a moment or two in order to pull himself back together as he had truly never felt more astounded. They started to ride along with the others with Osbert running alongside of them.

***

As they reached the camp, Kleo was completely stunned with all that Enzo had managed to build in such short time. She noticed that a few more ships had arrived at the island, which explained the number of guards that were roaming around. All the men seemed to be getting ready for battle and in the far end of the camp she got a glimpse of a few catapults right before she was taken to Enzo's chamber and the door was locked behind her.

Luckily, she was not locked up in there along with Enzo, and she was just pleased that they had not shoved her in a dungeon somewhere after her failed attempt to escape.

Besides two men guarding the door, she was all alone in the room. She could not help but become tempted to take a look around the chamber and go through Enzo's things, in case something useful was laying around in there just waiting for her to find it. The entire chamber was quite a mess, and the desk was full of maps and documents, it was a mystery to her how he even managed to keep track of where everything was. As she was taking a closer look at the documents on the table, she noticed a layout of the island underneath on a piece of parchment and next to it laid some wooden pieces where parts of the island were carved in. She took a closer look at one of the wooden pieces and realized that it could only be Hunter who had carved them. She clearly remembered seeing him carve something in wood exactly like the one she held in her hand at this very moment.

"That's how he found us," she mumbled to herself silently as she realized Enzo had been getting clues to their whereabouts all along.

She walked towards the window and looked out at the catapults that had been build. He was obviously preparing for battle, but against who? She wondered, for Enzo did not know about Elyas and the knights beneath the cave, let alone the dragon, or did he?

Kleo went back to his desk trying to search for more answers. Maybe he did know about the dragon after all. She looked through all the documents and, luckily, she found nothing suggesting that he had word of the dragon that was hiding in the depths of the cave, and she never got the chance to tell Hunter about neither Elyas or the dragon, so there was no way he could inform his father about it. Just as she was about to walk away from the desk, she noticed a drawn cross in the corner of one of the papers and it was identical to the one on Elyas' robe. She slowly took forth the paper in order to take a closer look. The paper did not consist of much but a few of Enzo's crooked handwritten notes, however, it was clear to her that Enzo knew about the knights on the island from what was written on it. She needed to get out of there, find Matt and warn Elyas not to end up in a war against him. With the number of men that Enzo had gathered, along with the catapults he had built, they were definitely outnumbered and would not stand a chance.

There was no way she was going to reach them back through the entrance to the cave, but according to the notes on the papers and the sketches, the knights supposedly had hidden tunnels beneath the surface. If she could just get out of there and find an entrance to one of their tunnels, she might be able to reach them in time. She tried to find more information and looked through everything one more time, just to make sure she had not missed anything important but was interrupted by the sound of someone on the other side of the door. She heard the guards talking to someone and the door was being unlocked. Quickly she dropped everything she had in her hands and tried to lay everything back on the table the way it was before, even though she did not exactly remember where everything was as she had not paid much attention to it until now. She walked away from the table just in the same second as the door got opened. It was Shirtless and Whitefoot entering the room. Kleo almost looked relieved to see who it was, maybe she had expected it to be Enzo.

"What do you want?" Kleo asked them as they were acting rather suspiciously.

They both just looked at each other and smiled without

saying anything and took a few more steps towards her.

"Stay away from me," she said, this time with a more serious tone to her voice hoping that it would make them scoot.

"You thought you were smart with your little escape back there," Shirtless said, obviously referring to when she had caused him to fall off his horse which she now could see that he was not too happy about.

"You got us into trouble you did," Whitefoot added as they walked in front of her, forcing her into the corner of the room.

"I'm sorry, I didn't mean for you to get into trouble," she said hoping that it would help the situation.

"Don't be sorry, you are about to get exactly what you deserve," Shirtless said while both of them grabbed her tightly around her arms.

Chapter Twelve

Matt, along with Osbert and the others, had almost reached the end of the tunnel. You could tell by the look on Matt's face that he was getting slightly nervous just thinking about the whole thing. Even though he was indeed a skilled swordfighter he had never been in a real battle before and he still could not help but wonder if Kleo was okay or not, or if he would even be able to find her. It was not exactly unlikely that they had already left the island. Elyas saw the worry on Matt's face, it was clear to tell that he was indeed a bit nervous, which was easy to understand given the circumstances.

"Do not worry, we will find her," Elyas said in an attempt to calm Matt's nerves.

In spite of Elyas's words, Matt did not seem convinced, however he still looked at him with a slight nod while trying to keep his mind in the right place. The tunnel got steeper, and Matt could tell that they were reaching what had to be the end of the long tunnel. He took a deep breath, and it was clear to him that they were now reaching the surface as the feeling of the air had changed just in the past few hundred meters. The air was less thick and felt fresher when he inhaled it.

A knight in the front gave a sign for everybody to hold. He, and two others jumped off their horses and walked towards a gate. It was not really a gate, it was more a huge piece of wood blocking the exit, followed by bushes and crates that they had to push aside so that they could get an easier passage through. Elyas looked at Matt checking to see if he was prepared or not. From the looks of it he seemed rather excited but also eager to get out into the open. Osbert stood right next to Matt's horse and kept a close eye on what was going on up in the front and his ears were stiff, pointing in the same direction as he was looking.

"Are you ready?" Matt said and looked down at Osbert who seemed to be very much aware that they were about to set foot outside.

His little tail started whacking and you could tell that the excitement was building up in his tiny body. Matt could not help but find it a bit amusing seeing the little guy so happy. Even Elyas could not help but smile as he saw the goofy little creature jumping around between the legs of the giant horses. The knights in the front had finally made clear passage and the sunlight from outside was rushing in through the dark tunnel and it was as clear as a lightning strike on the night sky. Matt squished his eyes together as the sharp light from the sun blinded him after being in the darkness for so long. All the knights began to slowly ride out of the tunnel and out into a forest. Matt, Osbert and Elyas were the last ones to get outside. As soon as they went through the opening Matt took a deep breath of fresh air and enjoyed the smell of the trees and flowers around him.

The sun was not too high in the sky and the night would soon be upon them.

"We camp here for the night," a knight said who was the knight that Matt assumed to be the one in charge, but he was not certain.

Matt helped the knights take the necessary supplies off the horses and set up camp. He was given the job of taking care of the horses making sure they were both watered and fed. While he was taking care of them the knights sat together going over their plan once more and Matt tried his best to listen in on what was said but it was not easy, given how far away from them he was standing. One of the horses began to be rather uneasy so Matt hurried over to see what was going on and tried to calm down the horse by holding one hand on its neck and rubbing it on the snout with the other. It appeared that Osbert had found the horses tail to be a good toy to play with, which had been making the horse nervous.

"Osbert, come here," Matt said.

"Kids," Elyas said with a chuckle behind Matt. He had walked over to make sure no danger was around.

Matt smiled to Elyas while kneeling down to pet Osbert and tried to make him calm down so that he would not disturb the horses further.

"It was Kleo's idea to bring him along," Matt said.

"She seems to have a very kind heart," Elyas said while kneeling down next to him to take a closer look at Osbert.

"She has," Matt said. "She is the kindest most loving person that I've ever met." It was clear to Elyas that Matt truly had strong feelings for her which he only thought to be a good thing.

Elyas looked at Osbert's body and gently opened his mouth to get a closer look at his teeth which Osbert did not seem to find soothing. "He is a very strong little one… he will prove himself to be a great and loyal companion."

Matt smiled and watched as Elyas got up and slowly walked away.

"Did you hear that, buddy? You are a strong little one," Matt said and winked to Osbert, before they too went back to the others. Even though he had not been supporting the idea of bringing him along in the first place, he could no longer deny that he had in fact grown very fond of him and indeed enjoyed his company.

***

Shirtless and Whitefoot were still in the chamber with Kleo. Just as Whitefoot threw a punch in her side right where her wounds were, Enzo entered the room.

"That's not how we treat our guests," he said which took the twins by surprise as they had not expected him to be back so soon.

They both backed away from her and she fell to the ground from the pain.

"Get out," Enzo ordered them and slowly approached Kleo.

"I'm sorry, they seem to have forgotten that we show our guests hospitality around here," he said while helping her off the ground.

"I'm not your guest," Kleo said while looking him dead in the eyes but Enzo, once again, seemed to not take her seriously and instead appeared to be rather amused by her words.

She bent forward from the pain and could barely stand up herself.

"My darling, you are injured," Enzo said and helped her to the chair. "We have to get that looked at."

Kleo sighed as she watched Enzo walk out the door and lock it behind him. She did not want to stay in his custody any longer than she had to, so she was trying to come up with a way to get a hold of his key. Enzo had only been gone for a few minutes before he returned, this time along with one of his men. She could hear them on the other side of the door, and she could also hear Hunter was out there.

"Is she all right?" Hunter asked his father.

"You need not concern yourself with her, now move along," Enzo said while opening up the door.

Kleo could see Hunter trying to look inside as he walked by, and she got eye contact with him for a quick second and realized that he most likely was her best chance of getting out of there. I would all be a lot easier if she could just get a chance to talk to him, which unfortunately seemed to be rather difficult as Enzo clearly tried to keep him away from her. Maybe he did not trust his own son. The guard and Enzo approached her, and they had brought bandages with them. The man had to be their physician or something in that major, at least she hoped that he was.

"You need to take that off," Enzo said and pointed at her leather corset. She removed it gladly as it was too tight from the swelling anyway and made it too hard to breathe.

She moved away from Enzo as he put his hands forth and was about to pull up her shirt. Just the thought of him touching her made her feel sick to her stomach.

"Don't be afraid, darling. I only wish for you to be well," he said and once again went to lift up her shirt, only this time she let him do so.

As he gently pulled up her shirt her almost black ribs were revealed. The man he had brought along took a closer look and asked her about the pain while examining her.

"You appear to have at least two broken ribs," the man said.

"Broken," Enzo said to confirm that he had heard the man correctly.

While the man wrapped bandages around her ribs in order to immobilize the area around them, Kleo noticed in the corner of her eye that Enzo was looking at his desk with an odd look on his face. She got nervous for a second as she thought he might notice that she had been looking through his papers.

"I see you have made yourself feel at home," Enzo said to

her rather suspiciously and walked outside while the man was finishing up the bandages.

She felt as if she had a big lump in her throat, maybe she had not put everything back in the right place after all.

"There you go," the man said and took the rest of his belongings and followed Enzo through the door. Enzo stopped for a second just as he was about to close the door behind them, he looked back at Kleo and said, "If you behave this time, I might even let you dine with me in the morning."

His words made Kleo rather uncomfortable, and she did not even get a chance to come up with a clever response before the door was locked.

Kleo took her shirt back down and stuffed it in her pants but left her corset behind since wearing it would only make the pain worse. She rubbed her eyes and tried to gather her thoughts. Outside, Hunter was not doing much besides pacing. He kept looking at the door to where Kleo was, arguing with himself whether or not he should go in and check on her, furthermore he was eager to explain himself to her and apologize for the wrong he had done. He had finally made up his mind and walked towards the door. As soon as he got a little too close the two men who were guarding the door, cut him off.

"You're not allowed in," one of the men said.

"Come on, you know me. I just want to see if she is okay," Hunter said desperately.

"It's your father's orders, I'm sorry I cannot help you this time," the man said. "You have to turn around."

Hunter had no option but to leave. He was clearly upset with his father's decision and was on his way to confront him about it. He scouted the area in search of Enzo, but he did not appear to be around. After walking around asking some of the men of his father's whereabouts he was stopped by Henry.

"What are you up to? Aren't you supposed to help out polishing the armors?" Henry asked him in a rather harsh tone.

"Yes, I just wanted to…"

"Wanted to what?" Enzo said. He had walked up behind them without Hunter even noticing.

"Why can't I see her?" Hunter asked his father.

"You know why," Enzo said and was about to move along.

Hunter grabbed his father tightly by the arm in order to stop him from leaving the conversation. Enzo stopped and looked furiously at his son.

"Hunter, let go," Henry said trying to stop the situation from evolving.

Hunter let go of his father's arm and stood back smiling as he watched both Enzo and Henry move along. Neither of them had noticed that Hunter had taken his father's key when he grabbed him, and he quickly placed it safely inside of his pocket.

The sun was setting and most of the men had gone off to bed and he knew his father was in Henry's chambers trying to find a way to open the chest. Only the men on lookout were around, besides Hunter, who was sneaking around trying not to be seen. He went to the house where Kleo was being held captive and intended to pay her a visit. He snuck around the back and started climbing onto the roof. Since he was not the best climber his climbing attempts accidentally made quite a lot of noise. Kleo who had fallen asleep in the chair was woken up by what sounded like a thunderstorm approaching but, as she got to her senses, she quickly realized that it had to be someone climbing on the roof, because thunder absolutely did not sound like that. She got up from the chair and got ready for whatever was about to happen. Hunter was on the roof and made his way to the front of the house. He knew there was no way he would get inside without knocking out the guards outside the door.

Without thinking further, he jumped down on one of the men and slit his throat with a knife and quickly knocked out the other with his elbow. He grabbed the key from his pocket and tried to shove it into the keyhole which was somewhat difficult since his hands were shaking from all the adrenalin in his body.

As soon as the door opened Kleo oddly enough found herself relieved to see it was Hunter in spite of her distrust of him, but she was also rather confused to see the two guards on the ground outside of the door.

"Come on. Quickly," Hunter whispered rather harshly.

She ran towards the door and Hunter grabbed her hand and almost dragged her out of there. They ran behind the building and sat down in the tall grass to hide themselves.

"What's going on?" Kleo asked.

"I'm getting you out of here," Hunter said and gave a sign for her to stay quiet.

He looked around, making sure that the coast was clear, and he then once again took her hand as they started running, guiding her towards the horses.

"You need to get to the forest," he said and pointed in the direction to where he wanted her to go since he knew she would be hard to spot over there.

"Why are you helping me?" she asked.

"I'm done being my father's errand boy," he said and looked into her beautiful eyes one last time.

"Go. Go now," he said and pushed her along, he did not want to risk being caught just for waiting another second for her to escape. After she went off, he slowly began to make his way back to his bed before anyone would get a chance to notice he was not there.

Kleo ran as fast as she could towards the edge of the forest and did not once stop to look back. Hunter was on his way back but could not help but stop to see if she had made it to the forest or not. As he turned around, he got a huge smile on his face as he watched her shadow disappear in between the dark trees and bushes, knowing that, for once, he had done the right thing.

Chapter Thirteen

It was a few hours into the night, and they were all asleep in the forest that was completely dark, only lit up by the moonlight shining down in between the trees. Everything surrounding them was quiet until leaves could be heard rustling in the distance , and whatever it was that made the sound was definitely approaching fast. Osbert, who was sleeping up against Matt's body, woke up from the sound and immediately started moving around restlessly, causing Matt to wake up as well. He too heard the sounds and got up in a hurry in order to check it out. Just as he was about to sneak away a voice started talking behind him.

"Where are you going?" a knight asked him. Matt's moving around must have woken him from his sleep.

"There's something out there," Matt replied and looked towards the sound and continued walking towards it.

The knight got up and followed Matt and Osbert. They went almost a few dozen meters into the woods whilst the sound became louder by the second and the knight accompanying Matt had drawn his sword. The knights shooshed Matt and stopped moving to listen closer to what sounded like someone moving towards them.

"It sounds as if it is only one man," the knight whispered.

Matt rested his hand on his sword handle in his belt. The noises were no longer to be heard so whoever it was had to be close by and maybe they had heard or seen them standing there in the middle of the forest. Both Matt and the knight looked around in all directions trying to see if they could get a vision of a someone moving around in between the trees yet nothing was to be seen. Osbert got the scent of something and immediately started following his nose towards a group of shrubs.

"Osbert, get back here," Matt whispered, but it was no use.

Osbert had clearly decided to walk over there and so he did. Matt carefully followed him, along with the knight who still had his sword ready for whatever was about to come at them. They all stood right in front of the shrubs and Osbert went straight inside of them and disappeared. Matt looked worried, where was he off too now? The knight stood still and gave Matt a sign to go around to the other side, so that they had a chance to cut off whoever was hiding there. Matt took a deep breath while trying to move as silently as he possibly could, but he accidentally rested his foot right on top of a bunch of old dry twigs causing them all to snap at the same time, which to his annoyance made quite a loud noise and got him to cringe his face.

He had almost reached around the shrubs when he heard a voice.

"Matt?" someone said and he clearly recognized the voice which immediately changed the look on his face.

"Kleo?" he almost shouted out of pure joy just before a shadow came rushing out from the bushes and firmly wrapped their arms around him giving him a huge hug. Matt closed his eyes, took a deep breath of relief, and simply enjoyed the fact that he had gotten her back, all while Osbert was jumping up and down around her being equally as excited to see her again as Matt was. Elyas had shown up in a hurry, along with two other knights, Matt's loud voice had woken them up as well. The knight that had been with Matt the entire time explained the situation while Matt and Kleo just stared at each other and smiled.

"I am pleased to see you are all right," Elyas said while they all escorted Kleo back to their camp so she could get something to eat and get some rest. On the way back Matt could not stop telling her about the magical forest he had seen underground inside the tunnels and showed her the armor that he was wearing, that he thought was really cool. She did not pay much attention to all the things he was telling her as she was too busy inside of her own head trying to remember everything that she had seen on Enzo's desk.

***

Back at Enzo's camp all hell had broken loose. The man that Hunter had knocked out had woken up, gotten back to his senses, and brought the event to Henry and Enzo's attention. Henry was investigating what had happened, but the guard had unfortunately not seen the attacker. It was clear that whoever had helped her escape had without a doubt had a key to the chamber since the door was left without a scratch and there were no signs of intrusion. Enzo was beyond frustration and let his anger out onto his men. He was not only yelling and throwing stuff around, but also pushing away everyone who got too close to him.

"Sir, she can't have gone far," Henry said in an attempt to get Enzo to calm down. Enzo looked at him with anger in his eyes as if he was not willing to listen to anything that anyone had to say. He looked around the room while thinking as hard as he could to get to the bottom of what had happened. His face changed in the second that he rested his hand in his belt loop as that is when it hit him. He looked down and noticed that his own key to the room was gone.

"Get my son. Now!" he shouted to Henry and punched his

knuckle onto the table.

"But, sir," Henry cautiously said.

"Now!" Enzo shouted once again, and Henry quickly left the room and hurried over to go and wake up Hunter from his sleep. Hunter's heart skipped a beat when Henry woke him up, he did not yet know if they knew what he had done or if they just needed his help.

"Your father is asking for you," Henry said calmly.

"What for?" Hunter asked, trying to act as if he knew nothing of what had happened during the night.

"He knows what you did," Henry said trying to see how Hunter would react to his words.

"What did I do?" Hunter asked him, still trying to act innocent while he slowly got out of bed and got dressed before they went to his father's chambers.

"Don't worry, I won't tell him," Henry said as he escorted Hunter over to Enzo.

Hunter was clearly concerned as he did not know what to expect, and he was unsure of why Henry seemed to know of his actions. The minute they reached Enzo he grabbed his son and almost threw him onto the table.

"What have you done!" he shouted in his face. "I know you had something to do with it!"

Hunter got frightened by his father and he was completely caught off guard.

"What do you mean? I haven't done anything," Hunter quickly said, hoping that his father would think it all was just a big misunderstanding.

His father punched him in the face hoping that he could scare the information out of him, but Hunter stayed quiet and took in one punch after the other.

"Sir, he is just a boy," Henry said, hoping that Enzo would stop hurting him.

"Leave, all of you, now!" Enzo shouted to Henry and the others.

Henry took a few seconds before he left the room, it was clearly difficult for him to leave Hunter behind, but he feared that if he stayed, he would be next.

Enzo stopped for a while, waiting for everybody to leave the room, while holding a firm grip on Hunter's shoulder, pushing him down against the table, which was clearly hurting him.

"How did you get my key?" Enzo threateningly asked his son.

"Your key? I didn't take your key," Hunter said in his defense.

"Don't lie, I know it was you," Enzo said and threw another punch, this time right into his son's abdomen, causing Hunter to gasp for air.

"I didn't take it," he said again.

Enzo stared into Hunter's eyes attempting to catch him in a lie, but it was too hard to tell, even for him.

"Maybe she took it when you were in here," Hunter said, striving to make his father doubt his own assumptions about his son's intentions.

Enzo stopped and let go of his shoulder, you could tell that he was thinking heavily as to whether or not it could be a possibility, and since he did not quite remember when he last saw his key, it definitely seemed as if his son's words could be true. Hunter stood up and adjusted his shirt which was all twisted around. Enzo kept his eyes fixed on his son and did not even blink.

"If I find out that you had anything to do with this, I will kill you myself," Enzo said while pointing his son in the face. Hunter was clearly frightened by his father and quickly ran out of the room before he could get harmed further. As he ran outside, he spotted Whitefoot and Shirtless who were occupied by burying the guard who had his throat cut. Henry was supervising the twins and saw how beaten up Hunter was, especially his face, he did not get to say anything to him before Enzo showed up outside.

"Do you want me to send some men out to find her, sir?" Henry asked.

"No, they'll be back," Enzo said and walked over to where the treasure was being kept.

"They?" Henry said to himself as Enzo walked away not knowing what he was on about.

***

Kleo sat around the fire next to Matt, with Osbert squeezed in between the two, and across from them was Elyas. She had been provided with plenty of food and water and was eating as if she had been starving for weeks. While filling her stomach with warm food she was in the process of telling them all about what she had seen on Enzo's desk, hoping that some of it might be to their advantage. She quickly understood, from all that Elyas had told her, that their plan was to retrieve the chest and force Enzo and his men off the island, but from what she had seen back at his camp they would certainly be outnumbered since Enzo had far more men than Elyas. In spite of her giving them that information, Elyas still seemed to be confident in their victory since his men were all respectable knights who had been trained to fight ever since they were all but young kids.

There were still a few hours until the sun would appear on

the horizon and a new day would begin. Elyas had gone back to sleep while Kleo and Matt remained awake for a little while catching up and just enjoying each other's company.

"Where's your corset?" Matt asked her with a hit of surprise as it had taken him quite a while to notice she was no longer wearing it.

"Oh, I left it behind when I escaped," she said and looked down at herself like she too had forgotten she was not wearing it.

"Why did you take it off?" Matt asked her confused as he had never seen her take it off, not even once. She did not say anything and just lifted her shirt up to show Matt that she was bandaged around her waist. He got a pale look on his face from the thought of Enzo having touched her but quickly shoved the picture out of his head since it made him feel sick to his stomach.

"Did they hurt you in any way?" he asked nervously and somewhat angry.

"No, no they didn't," she assured him giving Matt a moment of relief.

"How did you escape?" he asked her curiously but all she responded was "Hunter".

The expression on Matt's face changed as he tried to understand what had been going on at Enzo's camp, but he chose not to ask any further questions since he was afraid that he was not going to like the answer he would receive. After sitting there, next to each other, staring into the fire, without either of them saying a word, Kleo let out a big yawn. She was clearly exhausted from everything that had happened and needed to rest. She laid down next to where Matt was sitting and fell asleep in an instant. Osbert went over and laid by her side, and he too fell asleep in no time. Matt had too much on his mind so there was no way he would be able to fall asleep, even if he tried to do so. He remained awake and simply sat there next to the fire and kept an eye on her while she was sleeping.

The sounds of the forest were slowly returning, and you could tell that all the animals were beginning to wake up. The trees were full of owls that had been hooting all night long and now even the small birds were slowly starting to wake up. Close to their camp, Matt had noticed a herd of deer who were enjoying the fresh moist grass and did not seem to mind the presence of the knights and horses at all. He wanted to wake Kleo up so that she could see them, he knew her love for animals was rather huge, but she was heavily asleep, and he simply could not get himself to disturb her. Osbert, of course, had woken up as he could smell the animals nearby, and as curious as he was, he went closer and just sat on the ground to observe them. Matt had noticed the last few embers in the fire were disappearing and the sun was yet to rise, so he silently got up and went over to the horses and grabbed a blanket he had strapped to his horse's saddle, and then went straight over to gently place it on top of Kleo in order to keep her warm. He sat back down next to her, placed his elbows on his knees that were tucked in, while resting his chin on his arms as he watched the rays of the sun slowly peek through the trees as it was slowly rising in the horizon ahead.

***

The morning had finally come, and Enzo had Henry gather the men and have them suit up in armor and prepare their weapons. Hunter was helping out with the horses along with Whitefoot and Shirtless, who, to his frustration, used most of their time mocking him with his face that was all beaten up from last night. He never really liked the two of them very much and found them extremely obnoxious and they were always bullying him. They were neither skilled fighters nor very good guards, he knew his father only put up with them since they were related. As far as Hunter understood, Shirtless and Whitefoot were supposedly his cousins, even though he refused to believe he could be related to them in any way possible. Enzo was staring at the chest, he still had not been able to open it up which was really getting on his nerves. He grazed his hands upon it and walked around it a few times before he called out for Henry to enter.

"Sir?" Henry said as he walked inside, watching Enzo almost caressing the chest.

"Take a few men and have them load the chest onto my ship. I want it placed in my cabin," he said while keeping his eyes fixed on the chest. Henry nodded and was about to walk outside before Enzo stopped him.

"Do not under any circumstances let Hunter see that the chest is being moved," he said while staring Henry in the eyes.

"Sir," Henry said and nodded again and continued out through the door. He found Enzo's behavior strange but did not intend to confront him about it. He sighed, almost relieved, the minute he got outside as if he was glad to be away from him. Henry walked at high speed to where the horses were and grabbed Shirtless and Whitefoot to help him out with moving the chest.

"Where are you taking them? They're supposed to help me out with the horses," Hunter said.

"You can finish it up yourself, their help is needed elsewhere," Henry said to the boy and walked away without giving him any further information. Hunter continued his job and tried to look over his shoulder to see where the others were headed but they had already disappeared. He was very curious as to what they were up to, especially since Henry always informed him about everything that was going on, but not this time. He rushed to strap the saddle onto the horse he was preparing and got ready to sneak around to find out more information. He most likely would have succeeded if his father had not shown up out of the blue.

"Why haven't you finished yet?" Enzo said to him with a strict tone of voice.

"It takes time, and the others…" Hunter did not manage to talk further as his father cut him off and gave him a slap to the back of his head.

"Get done with it, now," Enzo almost shouted in his face. "And do something about that face of yours, it looks horrible," he said as he walked away in the same direction as the others had just gone. Hunter dared not speak another word and simply kept his head down and did his best to finish up the rest of the horses before his father's anger towards him would become much worse.

Chapter Fourteen

The mood was tense despite the morning being somewhat peaceful and all the knights were preparing themselves for battle. Matt had suited up in his chainmail, attached his bow to his back, along with his arrows, and had strapped his sword firmly to his belt. Kleo was the only one without armor which did not seem to comfort Matt in the slightest. Her ribs were still bruised but the pain had started to fade away, making it easier for her to move around which made her more confident about going into a fight. She had her sword, and that was all she really needed in the end.

"Osbert come here," Matt said, trying to have him stop making the horses nervous.

"Osbert?" Kleo said and laughed a bit.

"Yeah, I gave him a name. I thought he deserved one," Matt said and did not seem to get what was so funny about that.

Kleo just looked at him surprised and a little in shock and said, "I like it."

"What do you like?" Matt responded confused while trying to adjust his chainmail to fit a bit better in his belt.

"The name?" Kleo responded and laughed again from seeing the puzzled expression on his face. His mind was clearly everywhere else than present in their conversation.

Matt said nothing and just gave her a smile and was happy that she liked the name he had chosen. Kleo looked down at Osbert and called him by his name. He certainly seemed to like his own name as he got really over excited when she said it, or maybe it was just from the pets he was receiving, who knows really.

Elyas and the rest of the knights were ready to set out towards the beach, all of them were getting up on their horses and waiting for the command to ride out. Elyas took a look back at Kleo and Matt, who were in the middle of figuring out how to both get up on Matts horse. Elyas jumped down from his horse and approached them. Just as he reached them, they were both ready on the horse and Osbert stood on the ground ready to follow along.

"You do not have to follow us into battle," he said while looking at both of them with a look telling them that there was no shame in staying behind. They were both young and had a long life ahead of them and him and his knights could easily face Enzo on their own. Matt, who was sitting in the front, turned his head around and looked at Kleo for confirmation that there was absolutely no way that they would back out now. They both wanted Enzo to get what he deserved and they had not come this far only to back out now. Kleo smiled at him and nodded.

"We're ready to finish this," Matt said with confidence as he looked at Elyas who was now about to return to his horse and had an almost proud look in his face.

"Don't worry, everything will be fine. I promise," Matt said to her.

"Oh yeah, cause I haven't heard that before," she sassily replied and smiled to him.

They were all finally ready to ride out, and so they did. The morning was still young, and they had about half an hour's ride to the beach. They had all heard the plan and knew what they had to do, and since they wanted to take Enzo by surprise, half of the men would go around and approach his camp from the east, the other half from the west.

***

Hunter had just finished preparing himself to set out and now only needed to close the cinch on the saddle around his horse's belly. Whitefoot and Shirtless had returned from the ship and had been observing as Hunter had been struggling to prepare all the horses in time, while of course, giving him a hard time and mocking him the whole way through, not considering in the slightest to give him a helping hand. All the men had gathered, and each grabbed the reins of their own horse and were now waiting for orders from Enzo.

"The men are ready, sir," Henry said as he carefully approached Enzo who was in his chambers going over all of his maps and notes. He, for once, seemed to be pleased by what Henry had to say and quickly put down all that he had in his hands and prepared himself in his armor and grabbed his sword on the way out. In the very moment Enzo set foot outside, the otherwise sunny morning slowly began to turn grey from the clouds that were now gathering over his camp. Thunder could be heard in the distance and lighting strikes were slowly starting to cover the horizon. The storm was approaching fast, and raindrops had started to fall from the sky above them. Hunter walked towards his father and Henry as soon as he spotted them being on their way. He was towing two horses along with him, one for each of them. Henry immediately got onto his horse and thanked Hunter for bringing it to him, while Enzo almost tore the reins out of Hunter's hands and looked at his son with disappointment.

"Do not even think about letting me down if you value your life," Enzo said to him while pointing his finger in his face, again.

Hunter obviously got a bit frightened by his father and the furious look he had in his eyes. He was too intimidated by Enzo, so much so that he did not even answer him and instead just turned around and walked to his horse that was behind the rest of the men.

In the meantime, Enzo had gotten up on his horse and Henry was still next to him.

"Keep an eye on him," Enzo said to his uncle as he still did not trust him, and he truly considered his son to be spineless.

"Yes, of course, sir," Henry respectfully answered without questioning him in despite of almost seeming upset with his commands.

The men were ready to set out, and just as Enzo gave the order for them to ride out, an arrow came flying from out of nowhere and flew right past the head of one of his men. They were all taken by surprise and looked in every direction to figure out what was going on. Before they knew it a second arrow came flying, this time from the opposite direction, and this time the arrow hit one of the men in the thigh.

"Take cover," Enzo yelled, and the men split up, all riding in different directions, not really sure of where to go. The rain had started to pour down making it harder to get a clear vision and the waves in the sea were becoming taller by the minute. Henry spotted horse riders riding out of the forest from the left at high speed. He shouted out to Enzo who was not far from him, and he immediately spotted them as well. As the coward Enzo was, he turned his horse around in order to flee to the other side of the beach but was unfortunately met with the sight of even more riders approaching them from the right.

All the knights were wearing helmets beside Matt and Kleo who quickly caught Enzo's eyes. He almost got a glint in his eyes as he saw them and nearly had a smile on his face. Osbert was running in the back, behind Matt's horse, doing his best to keep up with them. Next to them was Elyas, he was supposed to have been in the other group of men but had chosen in the last minute to accompany Kleo and Matt, since he somehow felt responsible for them in spite of them being there by their own choice.

Shirtless and Whitefoot kept close to one another, and Hunter was riding right behind them. He was facing the men coming from the left, so he was nowhere near Kleo and Matt, or Enzo for that matter. Arrows were being fired from crossbows in the distance and landing all over the place. A few of Enzo's men were already on the ground and within no time the knights came clashing together with his men. The atmosphere was filled with the sound of thunder, swords rambling together and the whinny from the scared horses could be heard all around the beach.

Shitless and Whitefoot were approaching one of the catapults that had been built. Hunter was still trying to figure out who the hell they were fighting, and he deliberately tried not to lethally injure any of the knights and only wanted to disarm them. Hunter had no idea of what was going on so he was about to ride to find Henry, who was most likely to be found next to Enzo, and on his way to them he spotted Kleo who was standing on the ground in the middle of the fight. She had been pulled off of the horse by one of Enzo's men and Matt was still on the horse keeping close by and fought alongside of her. Osbert was hiding under some piled up wood pieces, staying dry from the rain, everyone but him was completely soaked from top to bottom. Hunter was halfway to Kleo when he noticed the twins in the corner of his eye and knew they were up to something. Everything inside his body told him to help Kleo out, but he decided that he had to stop Shirtless and Whitefoot from accomplishing whatever they were about to do. He turned his horse around and rode towards them as fast as he could, while continuously looking back at Kleo in the meantime.

He reached the twins who were just about to get ready to fire one of the catapults. He rode to the other side of it and cut the rope that was holding the arm with the payload. The arm fell down and neither of the twins seemed to have noticed Hunter. He smiled from seeing them struggle to comprehend what was going on and he quickly slit the ropes on the rest of the catapults before he rode along trying once more to get to Kleo.

Enzo was fighting alongside his uncle, fighting their way towards Kleo and Matt, who Enzo was eager to reach. Enzo reached out for Henry to pass him his bow and aimed it straight towards Matt. He fired an arrow that, unfortunately for him, hit Matt's horse instead of him. The horse fell to the ground and Matt went down with it.

Elyas had been drawn away from them but had seen what happened as he was still close by, and he now rode as fast as he could to help Matt get his leg out, that had been caught under the horse in the fall. Kleo was keeping Enzo's men away from Matt with the help from Elyas who took care of a few men before he was able to get a clear shot to help Matt, who was pushing as hard as he could to get free. All of a sudden Hunter came rushing over to Matt and helped push the horse away from him so that he could pull his leg out from underneath. He quickly got back up on his feet and looked surprised to see that Hunter was the one to help him out. Before Matt got a chance to say anything, one of Enzo's men came running towards both of them, ready to swing his sword at Matt. Hunter saw him coming and shouted for Matt to turn around and he managed to do so just in time for him to be able to block the sword that nearly hit him.

Enzo was still doing everything in his power to get through

to Kleo, but the knights stood their ground and blocked his way. He scouted for her and saw Hunter fighting alongside Matt, and he immediately got a furious look in his eyes.

The knights that had been approaching the camp from the left were having a hard time fighting off Enzo's men and it seemed as if they could really use an extra sword or two. Furthermore, Kleo had noticed that Shirtless and Whitefoot were working on the catapults, trying to get them up and running again and she knew they needed to come up with something if they were going to win this fight.

"Alvaro," Kleo said to herself and looked at Matt before she said the name to him as well.

Matt did not know what she was on about and kept his focus on fighting the guard in front of them.

"I know what to do," Kleo said and suddenly ran off.

"Stay here," she shouted to Matt while on her way towards a horse that was without a rider.

"Where else would I go?" Matt shouted back to her and shook his head before he pushed his blade into the heart of his opponent.

Kleo was calming down the horse who was completely stressed out and tried to get up on it. She got interrupted with Osbert who had run towards her.

"You have to stay here and look out for Matt," she said and finally got up onto the horse. She rode as fast as the horse could carry her into the forest from where they came. She almost felt as if she was flying, never had she been on a horse moving at such high speed. She was heading for the tunnel from where Matt and the knights had come. She went there only with the description of where it was to be found, that Elyas had told her the night before, and hoped with all of her heart that she remembered the directions correctly, as there was not a moment of time to waste.

Not much time had gone by before she reached the spot where the knights had made camp and where she bumped into Matt the night before, so she knew she was on the right track. Further ahead she reached a part where there was a huge tree with pink leaves, she clearly remembered Elyas had mentioned it, but whether she was supposed to go left or right when she reached it, she could not remember. She made the horse brake and stand still for a while giving her time to remember the way. Her gut told her she had to go left but she was doubting her own judgement. It was taking way too long for her to decide, and she truly did not have time to stand still. Without thinking any further she chose to go with her first instinct and rode off to the left.

The entire forest had started to build up with fog so she could no longer see more than a few meters ahead of her. The tunnel had to be nearby since she had passed a tree with two logs merged together, which was the last landmark before reaching the spot where the tunnel began. As she made her way in between the trees she carefully searched for the entrance which was nowhere to be found. The frustration was building up in her body and she was afraid she would not make it back in time. Just as she was letting the thought come to mind of turning back around, she noticed further ahead that the fog was moving rather strangely. It was as if the fog dropped further down to the ground or maybe it looked more as if it was being sucked down. Either way, it caught her eye and seemed odd, so she rode towards it to take a closer look. The frustrated look on Kleo's face immediately disappeared; she had found the entrance to the tunnel, finally. She took a deep breath and slowly rode inside.

The first part of the tunnel was somewhat steep, reaching

further underground and she was certainly surprised to see, not only the length of the tunnel, but also the size of it. It was indeed a huge tunnel, and she could not spot the end of it. She set up her pace and rode as fast as possible through the tunnel.

***

The storm was yet to be over and Enzo's men still appeared to be having the upper hand in spite of their catapults still not working. It had not been long since Kleo rode off and it appeared to have passed Hunter by. He was searching for her, it felt like not long ago she had been fighting right next to him, and now she was nowhere to be seen.

"Where's Kleo?" Hunter shouted to Matt, causing Elyas to react as well out of curiosity, as he too had not seen her for a while.

"She went to get help, I think," Matt shouted back to them. It almost looked as if Elyas knew what she was up to since he got a crooked smile on the lips and appeared to be getting more strength to fight back. Fortunately for all of them neither Enzo, nor Henry, had seen Kleo ride off into the forest as they were occupied with the knights being in their way.

"Where's the chest?" Matt asked Hunter while trying to shake off two men going at him at once.

"It's over there," Hunter shouted and pointed towards one of the small houses. Both of the guys looked at each other before they started to make their way over towards where the chest was being kept.

Just as Matt turned around to get moving, he was met by one of Enzo's men who stabbed him with his sword. Luckily it was not a lethal blow as it missed his heart and instead went into his shoulder. Matt fell down on his knee and the pain was close to unbearable. The sword had gone in quite deep and made a hole in his armor. Osbert came running, as if out of nowhere, towards the man that had injured Matt, and began to bite him in the leg and tried to drag him away from Matt. Hunter reacted fast and quickly approached in order to block the guard's next blow and it did not take long before the man was on the ground. Hunter helped Matt up on his feet and saw how bad his wound was.

"We need to stop the bleeding," Hunter said while placing one of Matt's arms around his shoulder to support and help him away from the battle.

"No, just get me to the chest" Matt insisted. Hunter did what he said and the two of them made their way across the beach to the building where the treasure was being kept safe. Osbert was right behind them and did not let Matt out of his sight.

When they were close to the house, Hunter found it a bit strange that no men were outside guarding the chest, but he quickly convinced himself that their help most likely had been needed elsewhere when he looked over his shoulder towards the battle. They had reached the door without being noticed and nobody appeared to be around so Hunter quickly kicked the door open, and all three of them rushed inside. The room was completely empty, and the chest was nowhere in sight. Hunter was clearly confused; he knew the treasure was supposed to be in there, but it was gone, vanished.

"They must have moved it," he said to Matt, who was trying to keep pressure on his wound.

Hunter realized that it could only have been Shirtless and Whitefoot who had moved the chest when they were ordered elsewhere earlier that morning. But where his father would have taken it, he simply did not know.

"Can you pass me that cloth?" Matt asked him and pointed to a piece of fabric on the floor. Hunter went to pick it up and gave it to Matt. He shoved it inside his chainmail onto the wound and put as much pressure on it as he could. While Matt was busy containing the bleeding, Hunter searched around for something they could use to support his shoulder but with no luck.

"You'll have to make do with that," Hunter said.

"Yeah, it's fine. Lucky it's not this arm," Matt replied to him and tried to smile and lift the arm he used to wield his sword. It was easy to tell by the look on his face that he was clearly in pain.

"You'll be fine," Hunter said before they both got quiet.

Osbert was in the corner and shook his fur that was soaked from the heavy rain outside. His fur got all fluffy and he looked like a furball, more than he did before at least. Both of the guys watched him do it and they could not help but laugh at him.

"I believe I owe you a thank you," Matt said to Hunter. He got surprised hearing those word from Matt's mouth and almost did not believe that he heard him right.

"You don't owe me anything," Hunter said and looked into the ground. Matt could tell that he felt bad about what he had done, and despite Matt not being fond of Hunter in the first place, he still could not help but feel bad for the guy.

"What happened to your face?" Matt asked him as he could not help but notice Hunter was all beaten up and they did not seem to be new wounds since the blood had already solidified. It got extremely quiet in the room for a few seconds as if Hunter was not sure of what to say back.

"When do you think Kleo will be back?" Hunter asked him to change the subject.

"I don't know, I don't even know where she went," Matt said. He was not sure if Hunter knew about the dragon, but he did not feel as if now was the time to bring it up, even though he was pretty sure that that was where Kleo had gone. They stayed inside for a while and while Matt was preparing himself to get back to the fight, Hunter was trying to think of where the treasure could have been taken.

"I think I know where it is," he said all of sudden and Matt looked up at him ready to hear the answer.

"It must be on the ship," he then said without knowing for sure, or which ship for that matter.

Matt looked as if he was about to give up from all the complications they kept facing. It was one thing after the other and there seemed to be absolutely no end to it.

Chapter Fifteen

Kleo had finally reached the end of the long tunnel and had managed to find her way through the maze, consisting of even more tunnels and passages, and was now making her way to the great cave where she would hopefully find Alvaro. Before she entered she let the horse wait outside, and as she went through the gate, she could feel her heartbeat getting faster and her thoughts were all over the place.

"What the hell am I doing?" she whispered to herself from realizing she might not have thought everything through.

She looked around but Alvaro was nowhere in sight, but then again, the cave was enormous so he could be hiding somewhere or be in the far end.

"Alvaro," Kleo cautiously called out for him. She waited for a while, but he did not show up.

"Alvaro!" she called again, this time louder, and the echo from her voice was heard all the way to the end of the cave and back.

After, what only felt like a few seconds, he appeared from behind a huge pillar and was flying directly towards her. She took a few steps back when he was landing on the ground in front of her, as she did not want to get too close in case he was not approving of her being there without Elyas present. After taking a close look at her it looked almost as if he bowed before her. Kleo stood completely still and observed his behavior carefully while thinking through what her next move should be. Alvaro leaned his head closer to her and she was not quite sure about what he was doing until she realized he was begging her for a pet or two. She could not help but smile as she laid her hand upon his cheek. He looked deep into her eyes and slowly blinked, showing her that she was not in harm's way.

"I need your help," she said to him. Not that she expected an answer in any way, but she was kind of hoping that he would somewhat understand her words.

They both just looked at each other for a while and the whole event began to almost feel awkward to her and she almost began to feel somewhat stupid for trying to conversate with a dragon.

"We don't have time for this, Alvaro, come on," she said and acted as if she was about to leave. To her surprise Alvaro followed her along and, in that moment, she realized that he had been waiting for her to lead the way the entire time.

She ran back to her horse with Alvaro by her side. They needed to hurry up and get back to the others as fast as they could if they were to reach them in time before it ended badly, assuming it had not already. The horse became startled as the huge creature came blaring towards it. Fortunately, Kleo calmed down the horse in no time and was ready to ride like the wind back through the tunnel with Alvaro right behind her.

***

Matt, Hunter and Osbert were back outside. The rain was almost over, and the thunder and lightning had gone. The sun was finally showing in between the clouds and the waves had calmed down in the sea. Shirtless and Whitefoot had almost repaired the catapults and Enzo was over there, along with Henry, getting ready to fire them. Matt wanted, more than anything, to find the chest and take it from Enzo, however, he could tell that Elyas and the rest of the knights were going to need the extra help from both him, and Hunter, so without further thought they made their way back to the fight.

The catapults were put into use once again, and before they had a chance to do anything about it, big rocks were smashing down from the sky hitting not only a few knights, but also some of Enzo's men got hit by the rain of rocks which he seemed unbothered about. Enzo put the twins in charge of the catapults and left their sight while dragging Henry along. It went on for nearly an hour with Shirtless and Whitefoot manning the catapults and if it was not for their bad aim and slow reloading, the fight could have already been over. Elyas kept looking back at the forest as if he was waiting for something or someone to show up and, before he knew it, he spotted Kleo, who came riding out of from in between the trees, faster than anything he had ever witnessed. Matt saw her too in the very second she had returned, and just as he was about to call out for her, he saw Alvaro flying across the sky.

"Sir," Henry said nervously to Enzo while looking up into the sky. Enzo's eyes became big and frightened as he too spotted the dragon.

"Stay here," he said to Henry and rushed away from there. On his way he picked up a handful of men, here amongst Shirtless and Whitefoot, to escort him away from the beach and towards his ship. Hunter had seen the dragon, and just as the rest of Enzo's men, he was, with good reason, having a hard time believing his own eyes and was obviously terrified.

Kleo called out for Alvaro and pointed towards the catapults, hoping that he would take them down. He flew above them and set them on fire before he landed on the ground and bashed the last one with his tail to the point where the entire catapult fell apart. Henry was looking for Enzo who was nowhere in sight. He called out for him until he saw that one of the ships had started to sail away into the ocean, and that is when he realized that they had been left behind and were now on their own.

Kleo had reached Matt and Hunter and both of them were more than pleased to see her, including Osbert who could barely contain himself. Kleo got a speculating look on her face as she noticed the bruises on Hunter's face, which she had failed to see earlier. In that very moment she dared not ask him where he got them from, as she was quite certain that she already knew the answer and was too happy to see that they had all gotten through in one piece.

"Lovely friend you have there," Hunter said referring to the huge dragon flying around.

"Yeah, he is pretty cool after all," she said and looked at Matt who agreed with her.

"Did you find the chest?" she asked both of them ready to hear some good news.

"We don't have it, but we know where it is," Hunter said.

"Where?" she asked him back quickly, being as ready as ever to go and retrieve it. Hunter said nothing, he just pointed towards the ship in the horizon and watched as her facial expression became, to some degree, annoyed, as she was watching the ship sailing far out into the open sea.

Elyas approached them as the fight was finally over, the few of Enzo's men that had survived, had surrendered themselves and kneeled in the sand.

"You did very well," he said and looked upon all three of them.

"Even you," he said and looked at Osbert with a grin.

"Thank you, but we've failed, and we lost the chest," Matt said, disappointed in himself that they had not gotten to the ship in time.

"You are a strong team; I am sure you will find a way around it," Elyas said encouragingly to the four of them.

Hunter walked towards the few of his father's men that had survived and surrendered. He almost felt happy when he saw Henry was among them. They had all dropped their swords to the ground and stood completely still since Alvaro was sitting in the sand next to them making sure they did not do any further harm. Hunter looked at Henry and tried to figure out what to say. He knew he had let them down, but he felt that he had made the right decision and chosen the right team.

"It's never too late to change sides you know," he said to Henry hoping that he would not scold him for what he had done. Hunter knew that Henry was a good and noble man at heart, he just needed to realize that himself.

"He is right," Elyas said.

Henry seemed confused and did not know what to say, and even if he knew, he was too afraid to say anything.

"How do we get away from this island?" Kleo asked as she had noticed, just like everybody else, that the rest of the ships at the shore had sunken. Maybe it was from the storm, and if not, they were all certain that Enzo had had something to do with it. Kleo looked at Elyas to see if he was thinking the same thing as she was, and she could tell that, without a doubt, he was indeed.

"Didn't you talk about a flying ship the other day?" she asked Matt and failed to keep away a big smile on her face from excitement as she looked over at Alvaro.

"No way, I'm not doing that," he responded quickly.

"Wait, do what?" Hunter asked, and did not seem to know

what they were on about.

It took him a while to realize what their plan was and as soon as he did, he almost panicked.

"I am not getting on that... that thing," Hunter said and pointed at the dragon.

"His name is Alvaro," Kleo said, causing the dragon to quickly get up on his feet, ready for whatever order was given to him.

Elyas could not contain his laugh from seeing the two guys faces. They really hoped that it was a joke but soon found themselves disappointed.

"It'll take him at least three days to get back, so we have enough time to get home and come up with a plan," Kleo said, hoping that the two of them would not back away from it now. The two guys agreed to use the dragon as transportation, since they did not exactly have any other options unless they wanted to stay behind and build a ship. Honestly Matt had already agreed in the very second she came up with the idea, he just wanted to get back at Enzo, and if it meant jumping on the back of a fire spitting dragon, so be it.

Since the sun was about to set, they had decided that it would be wise to wait until the morning to return home, because then they would also have time to attend to Matt's wound and get some food and rest as well.

***

An hour before the sun was up, all three of them had been woken up by noise coming from outside, they had been sleeping on the beach in one of the houses built by Enzo's men. The noise was made by Elyas and the other knights, who were busy taking care of the wounded and cleaning up the beach of corpses and dead horses who had to be piled up and burned.

Osbert was running around near the water playing with the waves that were gently washing ashore. Hunter was the first one to walk outside, he wanted to help out cleaning up the mess as he somewhat felt responsible for his father's actions, all the while Matt and Kleo went over to talk to Elyas.

"We're in great debt to you," Matt said. He knew they would not have achieved anything without the help from him and the knights, and he would probably not have seen Kleo again if it had not been for them either.

"You owe us nothing," he replied respectfully but thanked them for their offer.

"If you ever need us again, we will be there. After all, Alvaro is destined to be a part of your lives," he said, although neither of the two seemed to know what he meant by those words, but it probably had something to do with Kleo's father.

"Is it possible to open the chest?" Matt asked him, since not knowing the answer had been bothering his mind.

"It is possible, yes," Elyas said.

"But you don't need a key?" Kleo asked, believing that she might have figured it out.

"No, you do not," he said and had them patiently wait for him to continue talking.

"The chest itself is a puzzle, on the outside there are three green gems that look slightly different from the rest, you must push them and wait for a handle to appear. Once the handle is out you need to turn it clockwise until you hear the sound of moving gears. Only then will it be possible to press the purple gem on the top and the chest will open up by itself," he said while both of them listened carefully in order to memorize his words.

There was no way that Enzo would figure that out by himself so they knew that he would never find out that nothing of value was inside, which gave them the perfect opportunity to steal it back and have him believe that his efforts of becoming more powerful was gone.

"We should get going," Matt said and walked to Hunter having him get ready.

"I can't bring him this time; will you look after him for me?" Kleo asked Elyas, referring to Osbert who was still running around the beach.

"It will be an honor," Elyas said and bowed his head.

Kleo approached Osbert to say goodbye even though it hurt a lot to do so. Matt too went over to the little wolf who had proven himself a loyal guardian after all.

"Don't worry, you'll see him again," Matt said trying to comfort her.

"I know," she said, but still felt bad about leaving him behind.

It was time to leave, they had prepared themselves and were ready to get back to the mainland. They seemed hesitant to get on Alvaro's back, but with the help from Elyas, all three of them got up there in no time.

"Does he even know where we're supposed to go?" Hunter asked puzzled.

"He knows," Kleo confidently replied looking at Elyas who was standing proudly by their side.

"I hope this goes well," Matt said in doubt about how bad this idea could turn out to be.

"It's perfectly safe, I promise," she said and winked at Matt who shook his head and tried to hide his smile from her dumb jokes.

"There is nothing left for me to do but to wish you good luck," Elyas said and gave Alvaro a clap on the side so that he knew it was time to leave. As soon as Alvaro started moving all three of them got nervous and all grabbed on tightly and within little time they found themselves high up in the air, heading towards the open sea. They would lie if they said that it was not the most amazing feeling that they had ever felt, but at the same time also the scariest.

Osbert eventually noticed that they were leaving and attempted to catch up with them on the beach until he reached the edge of the water. He was clearly confused as to why he was left behind. Elyas went to stand by his side and watched the sunrise in the horizon while the little wolf was howling until the dragon was no longer in sight.

Chapter Sixteen

Today was the day that they would finally end this. Three days had gone by since they had reached the mainland and Alvaro had gone, most likely back to the island, without anyone spotting him along the way. The three of them had reached the village yesterday, and word had come out this very morning, that Enzo had returned. It was finally time to give him what he deserved, and they were more than ready to do so. They were very much aware that Enzo now had a shortage of guards since most of them had been killed in the battle and not many had returned with him and his ship. The possibility of them succeeding with their plan was quite big, or at least they felt comfortable that, for once, everything would go as they had planned it to.

They were on their way to his territory and went through all the narrow streets and walked in between the tall trees, as soon as they were out of the village, so that they would not be noticed along the way. If the chest was to be found anywhere, it would be there. Matt remembered the place from when they were first taken captive and, even though it had been somewhat dark, he still remembered the size of it, which was indeed huge. Where he would hold the treasure, they were not so sure about, however Hunter did after all know his father a little bit and assumed that he would keep the chest, either in his so-called throne room, or in the basement underground where he had other treasures locked away for safekeeping. But one thing he was certain about, it would be easier for them to reach the basement first, and if no guards were to be seen down there the chest, for sure, would be kept in the throne room upstairs.

It was nearly midday. They had arrived at his territory and were making their way to the back entrance, where they would find the stairway leading them underground. It was behind a wooden gate, that was to the left of an outer staircase, made of stone, leading to one of the towers used as a lookout. When the three of them arrived there appeared to be only one guard in the tower. He was walking back and forth scouting the area in all directions. They needed to time everything quite well if they were to make it to the gate unnoticed. They were on the other side, hiding in the bushes waiting for the right moment to get across one by one.

Hunter was getting ready to go first. Matt kept his eyes on the guard and would give a sign to Hunter as soon as the man had turned his head around. Immediately after he saw the sign from Matt, he ran as fast as he could and hid up against the wall next to the gate. Kleo was next, she got into position and was ready to run as soon as the sign was given to her, but the guard was on his way back so right now all she could do was to lay low and stay out of sight. She kept her eyes on Matt, waiting for him to give her the sign, it took a while but eventually there it was. She started running and accidentally dropped her dagger along the way. There was no time to pick it up, and she had to continue without it. She quickly reached Hunter at the gate and looked back at Matt and tried to notify him about the dagger on the ground. He did not seem to understand her hand gestures until he saw the guard in the tower looking down at the field.

Out of everyone, of course the guard had to be the one noticing the dagger, but yet how could he have missed it when it was shining in the sunlight being as visible as possible? There was no way the guard would turn around now so Matt needed to come up with an idea before the guard would, most likely, decide to check it out further, or worse, sound the alarm. The guard was about to walk down the stairs and if he reached the end, he would for sure see both Hunter and Kleo since they were almost standing right next to the end of the staircase. They could not see what was going on from where they were standing, all they could see was Matt looking all over the place, definitely seeming as if something was not right, and he kept giving them a sign not to move.

Matt grabbed his bow and took forth an arrow. He aimed it towards the guard in the tower and took a deep breath, he was very aware that he could not afford to miss the shot. He took in another deep breath of air and held it in while letting go of the arrow. It felt as if it went through the air for minutes before it hit the guard. It was a clean shot and the guard dropped to the ground without making any sounds. Matt exhaled and began to make his way across. Along the way he picked up Kleo's dagger from the ground and then safely continued and reached the others who were still waiting for him at the gate.

The gate was locked so Kleo wanted to see if she would be able to pick the lock. Before she got a chance to give it a go, Hunter kicked the door in, causing both gate and hinges to fall to the ground.

"That's not really staying quiet, is it?" Matt whispered to him in a rather feisty manner. Hunter looked at him, raised his eyebrows and shrugged his shoulders like it was nothing. Kleo just shook her head and went straight inside, letting the guys do their thing. She looked down the stairs to her right, listening closely if any voices were to be heard, or if the echo from footsteps were roaming the hallways, but all seemed quiet. Matt and Hunter had gone inside as well and were right behind her when she began to make her way down the stairs. In case someone was down there attempting to catch them by surprise, they all had their weapons in hand, ready to fight if it became necessary.

Soon they had reached the bottom and no guards were in sight. They walked down a big hallway, lit up by torches hanging on the walls, and silently made their way to the far end. Since no guards were around, they were certain that the chest was not down there, nevertheless they had decided to make sure and looked inside all the rooms anyway. Matt was mesmerized with all the gold and treasures locked behind bars inside almost every room they passed by. Enzo surely was a wealthy man; it was just a shame that he had been corrupted by his own mind in his lust for power instead of using his wealth for good. Many chests were down there but the one they were searching for was nowhere around. It had to be upstairs.

While making their way back up the stairs, you could see the nervousness on their faces from being so close to the end, wishing that it would all be over soon.

After being back at the gate, Hunter directed them down a hallway that led to the other side of the building. Here they would reach another set of stairs, leading up to the throne room. They were more than prepared and walked at a great pace through the hall, while of course, remaining as silent as they could. At the end of the hall, they heard two men speaking, they were around the corner, most likely standing on the stairs. All three of them listened closely and could tell it was Whitefoot and Shirtless, and maybe even a third guard was present.

Before walking around the corner, the three of them looked at each other confirming they were ready and gave each other a look of good luck. Hunter was in front and almost jumped out right in front of Shirtless, who was definitely taken by surprise, and almost stuttered before reaching for his sword. Matt and Kleo came forth only a few seconds later and went straight for Whitefoot. Before any of the three had a chance to stop the third guard, he ran up towards the throne room, went inside and closed the door behind him. The twins were fortunately not the most skilled swordfighters, and soon they were both wounded and down on the ground. Kleo rushed to the door along with Hunter and together they got the door opened in despite of the barricade that the guard had put up on the other side. They walked inside the room and saw Enzo along with two other men, guarding the chest. Matt entered the room only a little while later as he had been busy taking the arrows from Whitefoot's quiver.

Enzo did not seem happy about being reunited with his son, who he had strongly hoped would not have made it off the island.

"Well well, I should have foreseen this," Enzo said and looked at the three of them with a tormented look in his eyes. He gave a sign to his guards to attack and so they did. Hunter fought the first and Matt the second while Kleo went straight for Enzo, who remained alongside of the chest.

"I don't wish to fight you," Enzo said to her as she came at him with her sword.

"Good, that will make it quick then," she said back and struck her first blow, which was unfortunately a miss. Enzo kept blabbering on about her pretty eyes and how she should join his side, and he could tell as the strength in her blows with her sword became more powerful, that his words definitely made her angrier. Matt and Hunter were busy with the other guards and even two more had entered the room. One of which went to Matt and Hunter and the other went towards Kleo, giving Enzo a chance to retreat. It was clear that he did want to let the chest out of his sight, so he remained put, and seemed to almost enjoy watching the fighting in front of him.

The fighting went on and out of nowhere Shirtless and Whitefoot entered the room. They froze as they saw what was going on and Enzo called upon them for help. The twins looked at each other and then back at Enzo before they both fled the room like the cowards they truly were, and always would be.

The guard was about to hit Kleo with his sword and would have done so if Enzo's sword had not come in between and blocked it, which obviously surprised both the guard and Kleo.

"Look behind you, sweetheart," Enzo said.

She hesitantly lowered her sword and turned around. Both Matt and Hunter were held down by the other guards and their swords were on the ground in front of them.

"Last chance. Do you know how to open the chest or not?" Enzo asked, attempting to sound as polite as he could.

"No," she said, hoping that her words sounded trustworthy to him.

"All right then," Enzo said and was about to give a sign to his men to finish them off.

"Please no," Kleo said and approached the chest.

"So, you do know?" Enzo said intrigued and ordered the men to hold.

"Maybe," Kleo answered and walked behind the chest while trying to remember what Elyas had said. She did not do anything but look at the chest and was not sure of what to do.

"Come on now," Enzo said and rushed at her while raising his hand, staying ready to give orders to his men if she would not obey.

She looked at the chest and very much knew how to open it,

however, she was afraid of what Enzo would do when he saw what was inside of it.

She had spotted the three green gems and slowly pressed them one by one and, sure enough, the handle popped out. She noticed Enzo's face was filled with lust to finally get his hands on the treasure and she knew that within moments his look would turn to disappointment, or something far worse. She turned the handle as far as it would go and got ready to push down the purple gem on top. She looked at Matt with her eyes telling him to get ready to pick up his sword. She still had her sword in her hand and was prepared to kill the guard next to her as soon as she had pressed the gem.

She bowed down and placed her hand on the top of the chest and just as she pressed it, she yelled, "Now!" and both Hunter and Matt pushed the guards away from them, and each picked up their swords off the ground. Kleo had the guard on the ground and struck a lethal blow to his heart before she ran to help the others. All the while Enzo was so caught up with opening up the chest, that he did not have time to worry about the others. He opened up the chest and the very second, he saw a pile of old rocks inside of it, his eyes turned for a second into frustration, then into pure anger. He picked up his sword and almost ran to the others, yelling from the top of his lungs, and had only one thing in mind which was to kill Matt.

Hunter had seen where his father was headed and rushed over there to stop him. Hunter jumped in front of Matt, pushed him onto the ground and was met with a sword piercing through his back and straight into his heart, from none other than his own father. Kleo had not seen what happened as she was finishing off the last guard but she turned around when she heard Matt yelling and was met by the sight of Hunter falling to the ground. Enzo stopped for a second and took a few steps backwards as he almost did not believe what had just happened. He almost looked petrified from watching his son fall. Matt rushed to Hunter attempting to help him, and Kleo, who had still not realized what had happened, quickly made her way towards Enzo as she had seen her chance to finally finish him off.

"What do I do, what do I do?" Matt asked while Hunter's head rested on his lap.

"I don't think there's anything to do," Hunter said gaspingly.

"No there's gotta be something we can do," Matt said while trying to keep away his tears.

He could not believe Hunter, once again, had been there to save them, but this time in did not seem as if they would get the chance to repay him. Hunter did not say another word but looked over at Kleo who was fighting his father.

"Just hang in there, we will fix it," Matt said trying to stop the bleeding.

"It's okay," Hunter said. He had accepted his fate and was sincerely happy that he, for once, had chosen the right path, even if it had turned out to be a short one.

"I'm so sorry," Matt said and wiped a tear off his cheek.

"She loves you too you know," Hunter said while looking Matt in the eyes. He too had grown to care very much for her but knew in his heart that he would never have had a proper chance anyway. Matt looked at Kleo and tried to gather himself.

"Take care of her," Hunter said. And just then, he closed his eyes, took his last breath of air and was gone. Matt did not know what to do. Just as he was about to grab his sword and leave Hunter, he saw Enzo trip over the chest and land on the floor behind it. Kleo jumped on the other side and screamed from the top of her lungs as she pierced Enzo with her sword. His face turned pale, and he began to cough up blood. Kleo looked deep into his eyes and just stared at him for a few seconds.

"It's over," she said to him while he was begging her for mercy.

She ignored his words and backed away, leaving her sword inside of him. Matt called out for her and that is when she saw Hunter on the floor, looking as if he was asleep. Her heart stopped for a second before she ran to them. She fell to the floor and burst out crying. She was heartbroken from seeing Hunter lifeless and hugged his dead body as tight as she could. Matt could not bear to see her like this, he got up and went towards Enzo who was still conscious on the floor. He did not say anything, he just stood there and looked at him, almost feeling pity for the man, and he could not quite tell why.

"We need to bring his body and bury him," she said to Matt while the tears were still running down her face. Matt did not as much as flinch and kept looking at the disgrace of a man that was laying on the floor in front of him. Matt was out of words and grabbed Kleo's sword and pulled it out of Enzo's chest before he walked away from him and went over to help carry Hunter's body away.

As they left the room, Enzo was left all alone, sitting up against the empty chest alongside of the last of his men that were lying dead on the floor around him. Enzo's eyes had the look of panic in them, it was clear that he was scared, and he fought his best to get back up on his feet but with no luck. The strength of his arms was failing him, and he could feel his heartbeat becoming weaker with every breath he took. The color of his skin turned paler every second and he was struggling to stay awake. He made a few attempts to call for help, hoping that Matt and Kleo would walk back into the room and spare his life. The sunlight appeared through the window and Enzo could feel the heat of the sun against his face.

That was where he sat, thinking of how his lust for power had made him kill his own flesh and blood. And that is where he took his last breath, and his soul slowly left his body.

Six months later

It was spring, and all the trees and flowers were finally blooming again. The village had come back to life after Enzo and his men were gone, and the treasures and gold from his fort had been taken by the king and the riches had been divided upon the surrounding villages and were used to restore everything that had been vandalized. Shirtless and Whitefoot had not been seen since they had fled from the fort, so wherever they had gone it had to be far away from the kingdom.

The live music was once again heard throughout the streets and the children playing on the streets had too returned. Matt was back helping out in the toy maker's shop and Kleo was once again helping her mother in her stall at the market. They were both considered the heroes of the town, and in the villages surrounding them; however, they did not see themselves as heroes. They would not have gotten far on their quest if it had not been for Hunter, who they still mourned.

They had buried him on the top of a hill in the meadows, underneath an old ash tree where daffodils grew all around. Stories had always been told of how they represented new beginnings and rebirth so they could not have thought of a better place for him to rest.

Usually, they went up there once a week to visit him, telling him about what trouble they had been up to in the meantime or simply just sat there and enjoyed the view. Today they had decided to pay him a visit and watch the sunset from the hill. The mood was always strange whenever they went there, on one hand they were still grieving Hunter and both of them, especially Kleo, were missing him a lot, but on the other hand they could not help but feel relieved that they had gotten through it all and that it was finally over.

***

They had reached the top of the hill, and both stood for a minute in silence while looking upon the cairn they had built on top of the grave. There were still a few hours until the sunset would appear across the sky so both of them went and sat underneath the ash tree and waited. They sat talking for a while and soon noticed something moving in the meadow, they could not quite tell what it was, but as soon as they heard a howl they knew, or at least Kleo seemed to know.

"Great, now there's wolves around here too," Matt said, somewhat unenthusiastic.

Kleo did not say anything and looked down to see if it could really be. She got up and began to make her way down the hill.

"Kleo, where are you going?" Matt said and jumped up to follow her, even though he did not quite want to. She said nothing and continued making her way down the hill.

"Kleo, we shouldn't go down there," he said again before he tripped over himself while almost running to catch up with her. He tumbled around for a few seconds before he got back up on his feet and tried to act as if nothing had happened and was brushing his clothes while trying to keep up with her.

"That's not possible," she mumbled to herself and ran the rest of the way down. She could hardly believe her eyes and was sure for a minute that they were deceiving her.

It for sure looked like Osbert running towards her, and so it was. He was all grown up and was indeed a massive wolf now. As she reached him, he jumped around her and was truly excited to see her again. Matt came along as well and was equally as surprised as Kleo was. Osbert went towards him and begged for as many pets as he could get away with.

"But if you're here that means…" Kleo did not finish her sentence as she looked up and spotted Elyas further out alongside another knight.

"Matt look," she said, and he neither could believe who he saw in the horizon. They walked towards them and Osbert, of course, followed suit.

As they got closer, they could tell that the knight at Elyas's side, was Henry. Now that, they would never have guessed.

"I can't believe you are here," Kleo said and greeted Elyas. Before Elyas had a chance to greet Matt he went straight for a hug, which caught Elyas by surprise, but he could not help but smile.

"What brings you here?" Matt asked after he was done hugging him.

"I am here because I am in need of your help," Elyas said and at the same time his face turned somewhat serious. Matt and Kleo could not believe it, first of all they did not expect to ever see him again and furthermore he even wanted their help. Both Kleo and Matt had been eager for a new adventure since working in the village did not quite sooth them any more, however, this had never crossed their minds. They looked at each other with fire in their eyes almost as if they had decided to say yes before knowing what it was all about.

"It will be dangerous, and I cannot promise you that you will return," he said.

"We are ready," Matt said confidently and without the slightest of hesitation.

***

That very same night they met up with Elyas and Henry on their ship, along with Osbert, and the rest of the knights, where they once again were to sail out into the open sea. Kleo was enjoying the view of the sea before they were to board the ship and she was eager to jump in for a quick dip. She had finally pulled herself together and learned how to swim and usually went for it at every chance she got. She could not help herself and chose to jump off the edge of the harbor and straight into the water with Osbert following suit.

Matt and Elyas were already on deck and were looking at all types of different old maps that all appeared to be drawings of parts of an island. They were not going to the same island this time, which many others have still tried to locate to this day and failed. This time their quest was further away where almost no man had ever set foot and where peculiar things were said to occur. Kleo and Osbert had made their way onto the ship and were ready to set out. Osbert shook his fur which caused him to turn into a giant ball of fluff, which Kleo could not help but laugh about. Matt heard her lovely laugh behind him and turned around to see what had made her so happy and he obviously could not help but let out a chuckle as well when he saw Osbert with his new hairstyle.

The captain of the ship gave out orders to the crew and they finally left the shore. Kleo was playing around with Osbert on the deck, all the while Matt and Elyas stood at the front of the ship and scouted out into the open sea watching the sun slowly setting ahead of them.

Henry was helping out keeping control of the sails as the wind was getting heavier the further they got from the shore. It was still odd for both Matt and Kleo to see him as a part of the knights and he definitely had to earn their trust, given the circumstances of what had happened in the past, nevertheless they could tell that he seemed to have found his place and if Elyas trusted him, they had to try to do so as well.

"Where are we going exactly?" Matt asked Elyas since he had not yet revealed where they were off too.

"25°N 71°W," he said as their ship disappeared in the horizon and could no longer be spotted from the shore.